I0721439

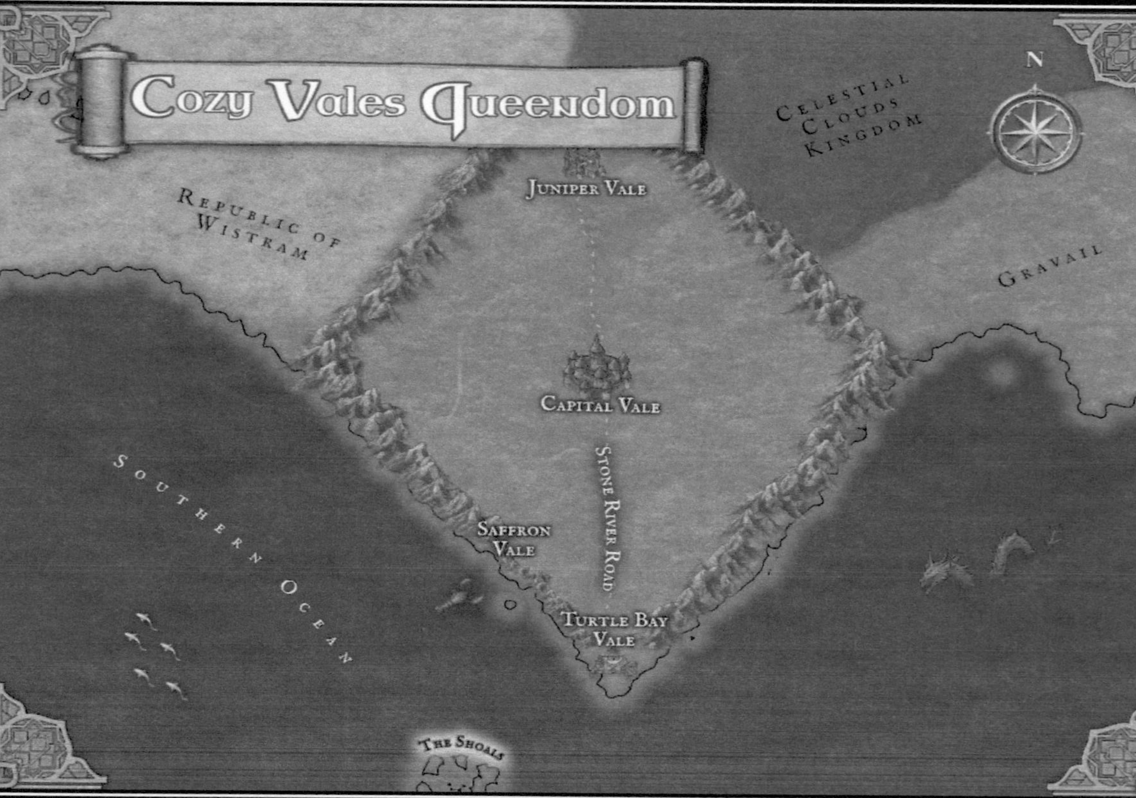
Cozy Vales Queendom
Celestial Clouds Kingdom
N
Republic of Wistram
Juniper Vale
Gravail
Capital Vale
Stone River Road
Saffron Vale
Southern Ocean
Turtle Bay Vale
The Shoals

Saffron Vale
N
Rainbow River
Cheese Rolling Hill
Dyeing Pools
Crocus Fields
Woolton
Hot Springs
Great Lobster Cove
Southern Ocean
Wyrm Rock

Saffron Vale Series – Book 1

A Colour to Dye For

A Cozy Vales Story

G Clatworthy

2 3 4 5 6 7 8 9 10

ISBN: 978-1-915516-42-8

© Gemma Clatworthy 2024

Find more at *www.gemmaclatworthy.com*

AI Training Prohibition: Unless stated otherwise, the author holds any and all exclusive rights to the entire content of this book, A Colour to Dye For. Any use of this publication to develop and "train" AI software in any way, for any reason, is expressly prohibited. No generative AI was used to produce this book.

This book is based on the Cozy Vales world and content created by Raymond Walker

https://cozyvales.com

The moral right of Gemma Clatworthy to be identified as the author of this work has been asserted in accordance with the Copyright, Designs and Patents Act of 1988. All rights reserved. No part of this publication may be reproduced, stored in a retrieval system or transmitted in any form or by any means, electronic, mechanical, photocopying, recording or otherwise, without the prior permission of the copyright owner of this book.

This is a work of fiction. All characters and events portrayed in this book are fictional and any resemblance to real people or incidents is purely coincidental.

Cover art by Get Covers.

Foreword

A massive thank you to the Cozy Vale scribes who read this and provided all the support and encouragement in creating Crimson's story. This wouldn't exist without you.

A special thank you to my amazing typo hunters, grammar gurus, and plot pickers who got this story to where it is today. You are awesome!

If you want to support Gemma, you can find her on www.patreon.com/G_Clatworthy for exclusive first reads of new stories. You can also join her newsletter at www.gemmaclatworthy.com for a free short prequel to the Saffron Vale series and follow Gemma on www.instagram.com/gemmaclatworthy,

www.facebook.com/gemmaclatworthy or join the reader's group on Facebook: Gemma's book wyrms.

An extract from Intara's Guide to Cozy Vales –
Highlights and Summaries of my Time in the
Queendom

Saffron Vale is named for the crocus flowers that grow there. It is known throughout the queendom for its brightly coloured cloth and excellent dyes. It is unsurprising, then, that its local cuisine includes spices that add colour as well as flavour and I implore you to try the yellow saffron cake – a yeasty cake stuffed with currants and other dried fruits that is a buttercup yellow colour.

I first tasted this delicacy in the Cozy Lobster café in Woolton – the main town in the vale – where I also sampled a half-moon shaped savoury pastry called a 'pasty' (pronounced colloquially as 'paasty', which was both filling and delicious.

You may well choose to pair it with scrumpy – an alcoholic apple drink that is well known in this vale. Each orchard here has its own recipe, and the drink varies in taste from sharp to so sweet you would hardly guess it contained alcohol.

When I inquired about the name of the café, I was told it was named after a great lobster who has visited this vale since time immemorial, but though I wandered through both Lower and Upper Gull's Bottom – once a small village, now part of the outskirts of the town – to the beach, I didn't catch a glimpse of this famous visitor.

Another export is the rainbow trout, a fish native to the river that flows from the mountains in this vale right to the sea. It is said that the scales are so colourful as a result of the hues that leak into the river as part of the dying process. This seems to do no damage to the fish or local wildlife except to imbue them with colour. One of the best sights in this vale is the elusive rainbow river that occurs when conditions are just right and the dyes, instead of combining in swirls, flow instead in almost straight lines down the river. I was fortunate enough to witness this event during my visit and can confirm that it is indeed glorious.

On my way out of the vale to my next stop, I rested at the small hamlet of Innton. As you might expect from the name, the most notable feature of this town was the large inn. Other than the extortionate prices, there is nothing else to say about this place, so I shall move on.

Intara's Guide to Cozy Vales – Highlights and Summaries
of my time in the Queendom

Chapter 1

~ *Disappointment and danger* ~

ULL.

That was the first word that popped into Crimson's head as she surveyed the sprawling valley below her. It was an unappealing description for the vale she had pinned all her hopes and dreams on.

For a brief moment, she contemplated heading back to the travelling library that had brought her to the bottom of the pass. The library moved at a glacial pace in a zigzag route across the queendom, and she would catch up with it soon if she hurried.

But what life was for her there? The caravan was big enough for sitting, mending books and, of course, reading, but not suitable if she wanted to create clothes. And she did. That was why she'd left her home in Oasis, why she was here.

Saffron Vale was known for its bright dyes and yellow and purple crocus flowers. Crimson consulted the guidebook. Yes, there was the colour illustration that showed a field carpeted with the beautiful blossoms under a bright sun. If someone had to illustrate the word picturesque, this drawing was a contender for the top spot.

Crimson peered over the book and back at the valley. Grey clouds scudded through the sky, getting darker in the late afternoon. No blossoms of any kind penetrated the green fields. A sheep bleated somewhere in the distance.

No matter. Perhaps they kept the crocuses – croci? – somewhere else. Crimson forced a smile onto her face and took her first step into her future.

Raindrops spattered the ground. Typical.

But she was determined to be positive and so picked up her pace as she headed down the winding track that led to the large town of Woolton.

An hour later, her travelling cloak was soaked, its emerald green turned to a darker shade that was closer to pine or perhaps spruce, and a coating of mud stuck to her boots. She was also lost.

Crimson squinted down the road, unable to see anything but trees in front of her. The large, well-maintained paving of the Stone River Road that stretched from Juniper Vale in the North to Turtle Bay in the South of the queendom had long since disappeared into narrower, muddier tracks.

She frowned and took out the guidebook. Rain splattered its illustrated pages, so she put it away before the ink ran. Nothing for it. She headed into the forest that sprawled a little way from the path.

At first, the respite from the rain was a welcome change, and she lowered her hood to better take in the dark woods. But soon the strange sounds of the trees unnerved her. Every gust of wind sent the leaves rattling and whispering as if they foretold her doom. A crack of a twig made her spin round, clutching her bag, heart pounding, ready to run, but there was nothing there.

Above her, the canopy darkened, blocking out the meagre light along with the rain. She clutched her bags closer as the forest pressed in.

A bramble snagged at her dress. She freed it and sucked her finger as blood beaded where the sharp thorns bit into her flesh.

She continued on, moving over the forest floor with clumsy footsteps as every fallen leaf and twig stuck to her muddy boots. Soon, the path dwindled into a dirt track then into nothing. That's alright. She merely had to retrace her steps, and she'd be back where she started.

Crimson turned and realised she had left the path long ago. She was alone, lost amidst trees that rattled in the growing storm, with no idea which way to go.

The tears that had built up in her eyes welled over, tracking hot paths down her cheeks. Despair spiralled through her. She had pictured her triumphant entrance into the vale of her dreams and its town in a hundred different ways and not one of them had included rain so thick she couldn't see more than a couple of feet in front of her or getting lost in sinister woods.

A wolf howled; its voice muffled in the thick forest.

Crimson pressed herself against a tree, holding her bags up in defence against the wild creature. She wiped away her tears to clear her eyes. Crying wouldn't do any good. Even if this was the end.

Her breath came in shaky gasps as the wolf howled again, further away this time. Or was it? Maybe the trees hid its location, and it was right behind her. Crimson spun, her eyes searching for any movement. She was going to die in the woods outside of Woolton. No one would even know she was here, and she'd meet her end in a muddy hollow somewhere.

Her fingers felt in her pocket for her mother's thread on its wooden spool and she rolled it in her palm, feeling the shiny silk. It was her good luck talisman. Crimson sank to the floor and leaned against a tree, moss covering the rough bark in a vibrant shade of green, closer to fresh-cut grass than deep mossy green. Her mother's favourite colour. Was it a sign she was on the right track? She plucked some of the springy plant and rolled it between her fingers. If she survived, this would make a gorgeous colour for a dress or overcoat. But it didn't matter because she couldn't find her way out of these woods.

Perhaps they were enchanted…the thought crossed her mind like an errant breeze. If there were teg folk in here, she could claim kinship – if they'd accept a half blood – and, of course, that depended on there being anyone else crazy enough to be out in this weather. Did tegs even like the forest? She knew so little about her mother's people.

"What are you doing here?" A deep male voice interrupted her brooding.

Crimson looked up at the hooded figure that stood opposite her. Where had he come from? Was he friend or fiend? She licked her lips, moistening her dry mouth, and decided to tell the truth. He might be her only way out. "I'm lost."

"I can see that. Why are you in the woods? No one comes here in a storm."

She took in the long knife slung from his belt before he covered it with his cloak. She shoved herself to her feet and pressed her back against the large tree. "You should know I'm armed."

The stranger crossed his arms, somehow projecting amusement. "I can see you're more than a match for the wild beasts of the forest. Have a good day." He turned his back on her and strode off, following some path that Crimson couldn't see.

"Wait!" Crimson's gaze darted between the trees. The man halted. "What sort of beasts?"

"A few bears, the odd unicorn, that sort of thing."

"Unicorns aren't vicious," Crimson scoffed. "There were two pulling the library I travelled with."

"Mixed breeds. Or maybe a different type. The unicorns round here are nasty pieces of work; they'll kill you as soon as look at you. What do you think the horn is for?"

"You're joking with me."

The man shrugged. "They're territorial." He shot her a look. "They know when someone doesn't belong."

Crimson squared her shoulders. "Will you help me find my way to Woolton?"

He stayed silent, appraising her and she got the impression that she didn't measure up.

"Please." Her voice broke.

"Fine." He lingered on the word, making it sound like she was an imposition. "Keep up."

"Thank you." Crimson scurried over to him and held out her hand. "I'm Crimson, from Juniper Vale originally, I'm on my way to Woolton to–"

The man brushed her hand away. "I don't need your life story. Let's get a move on before anything catches our scent."

"Right, of course. Let's go." Crimson took two steps forward and collided with the man's broad back. "What–?"

"Stay quiet," he hissed.

"Why?" she whispered back, stepping around his body so she could see what had caused him to stop. A magnificent, dappled unicorn stood blocking their route. "A unicorn? That's why we've stopped? It's beautiful."

"Be quiet!"

Crimson closed her mouth and studied the beast in front of them. This close, she could see a number of differences between this unicorn and those that had pulled the travelling library. Size was the obvious thing that came to mind; this unicorn was half as tall again as the sturdy horse-like creatures who had pulled the cart. But there was something else too…

This unicorn's eyes brimmed with intelligence. It snorted at them as if the two people standing in its way were nothing more than an inconvenience.

This was a creature who knew it was on top of the food chain and it knew who counted as prey. Crimson swallowed. Sweat pricked along the back of her neck. She stepped back. A twig cracked under her boot.

The unicorn lowered its head and charged.

Chapter 2

~ What's so great about the country? ~

THE MAN SHOVED CRIMSON to one side, and she went sprawling onto the soft leaf-covered forest floor, pinned under his heavy body. All breath left her lungs, and she stared up into a hard pair of eyes.

Remembering herself, she lowered her gaze to study a scar that ran along the edge of his jaw, hidden beneath his stubble, before he took note of her rainbow-flecked irises that marked her as one of the teg folk and decided not to help her.

He muttered a curse about 'ruddy outsiders' before he jumped up, leaving her on the ground as the unicorn pivoted, whinnying its frustration.

It scraped a front foot on the ground and eyed the man with menacing intent. But instead of running or taking any action that a sane person might, the woodsman squared up to the enormous beast, waving his arms and shouting something in a language Crimson didn't understand.

The beast charged again, its pointed horn glinting in the half light.

Repeating the strange words, the woodsman stepped forward, holding his ground, arms splayed out like he was herding a stray dog and not this murderous beast.

And, unbelievably, the unicorn skidded to a stop in the mud just before its horn gored through the man's body. It pawed at the ground, snorting.

Crimson let out a cry of surprise.

The unicorn reared up, black hooves pawing at the air. Just one of the giant hooves could crush a man. Crimson screamed.

The woodsman stepped to one side, taking a glancing blow from the hooves of death that knocked him to the ground.

The unicorn snorted once more, then turned and galloped off into the forest.

Crimson scrambled over to the man's side. "Are you hurt? What can I do?"

"You can leave well alone. I told you to be quiet, and you screamed. Somebody could have got hurt."

"There's no shame in being injured. Come, let me see if I can help."

"You've done enough." He shoved himself to his feet, leaving Crimson crouching in the dirt. "Come on. And next time I tell you to be quiet, listen."

Crimson found her bright yellow ribbon and retied her hair before getting to her feet and grabbing her bags. She followed in silence, hugging her cloak to herself. A gentleman would offer to help her, but it was clear this man was anything but gentle. He faced down rogue unicorns in the wild. Crimson wrinkled her nose. And he probably didn't bathe.

A few minutes later, and Crimson couldn't help herself. "So, are there lots of unicorns in the forest?"

"Some."

"And what about bears?"

"More."

"And…wolves?"

He turned at that and gave her an impenetrable stare before setting back off again.

"You don't talk much, do you?"

"Shh." He held up his hand. Crimson froze.

"What is it?" she whispered.

The man continued walking, picking his way among the trees as if he followed a secret path that lay there, invisible to her eyes. The oak leaf badge pinned to his cloak winked as it caught the dappled light that made it through the canopy.

Crimson frowned as she hurried to catch up with him. A suspicious thought scurried across her mind. "There's nothing there, is there?"

The corner of his lips twitched.

"You just want me to be quiet."

"Yes! Finally, you get it! There's a reason I moved to the woods."

"Oh?"

"To be away from people like you."

"People like me? What does that mean? I'm a delight."

"You're an outsider, from a city." He shuddered at the last word like it was an evil place that had the power to frighten grown men.

"So? There are nice people in cities."

He huffed out a snort of disbelief.

"What's so great about the country, anyway? There's mud and dirt–"

"Those are the same thing."

"And rain. And wild animals."

"Why did you want to move here then, if you hate it so much?"

His question shocked Crimson into silence for a little while. "It's complicated," she said eventually.

The man nodded but didn't probe further and they continued along in a sort of companionable silence for a while, heading down the sloping forest floor.

"What's that smell?" Crimson's nose crinkled at the stench that grew stronger as they walked through the woods.

"Woad balls."

"I beg your pardon."

"Balls. Of woad."

Crimson frowned as the combination of rotted cabbage and sewage filled her nose. "Does every animal in the forest use them as a latrine?"

"The dyers leave them here to rot down. The wind blows the smell away from town." Was that amusement that made his lips twitch?

Crimson held her dress over her face as they passed the stinky balls of rotting leaves.

"And this makes dye?"

"It's part of the process."

"And the other part is?"

The man stayed silent.

Crimson narrowed her eyes. "You chose this route on purpose, didn't you?"

That slight twitch of his lips again. The man was maddening. Well, if he thought he could deter her, he was wrong. Yes, she'd had a slight hiccup earlier, but who could blame her? She had been lost and alone. Now, back on the right path, not even fermenting balls could deter her.

The trees were thinner now and a twinkling light caught her eye, then another.

Her step quickened as they neared civilisation and hope.

It was hard for her shaken heart not to plummet again as they paused on the edge of the forest, looking out at the pelting rain and the grey town that squatted in the valley like an unloved creature. It was not the centre of bustling activity that she had hoped for, and it was nothing like her previous home.

Instead of neat, orderly buildings arranged in rows, Woolton appeared to have foregone any sort of town planning with dwellings placed in a haphazard fashion wherever the residents fancied building them.

Back in Oasis, the buildings had stretched towards the sky seeking light and space in the tightly packed city. Here, the houses and shops were two storeys high, maybe three at the most, as if the coastal weather damped them down.

A light winked in the distance, a pinprick in the thunderous clouds. Crimson squinted.

"There's the town." The man turned to go.

"Wait, please, who should I see?"

"About what?"

"About renting a property."

"Council."

Crimson stood waiting, but he didn't expand on his single word answer. Biting back a retort about how infuriating the man was, Crimson instead coated her voice with sugar. "Perhaps you would be good enough to show me where the council offices are, as I'm new to the area…" Her stomach rumbled. "Or maybe you could point me towards a local eatery. I'd love to get the authentic Saffron Vale experience, I adore the saffron cake from round here."

"Authentic experience?" The woodsman lifted his eyes to the heavens, sighed as if the weight of the vale was on his shoulders and then said, "Fine," before heading out into the rain.

With a smile, Crimson followed him, gripping her cloak tight around her body as the wind lashed at her.

She could barely take in the town as the man set a quick pace, as if he wanted to get back to his trees as quickly as possible. They hurried past a street name – did it really say 'Upper Gull's Bottom'?[1]

Crimson kept her head down against the driving rain and so it was a total surprise when they stopped.

She squinted around, trying to make out anything in the downpour. A squat building hunkered against the storm while waves lashed the nearby beach and tossed the boats moored against the spindly jetty like they were toys in a bathtub.

Rich candlelight streamed through the small windows and a battered sign sporting a picture of a white gull swung in the wind. The murmur of people enjoying themselves and a tinny tune wafted out of the building.

"Drunken Gull. Best authentic pub in the town."

Crimson thanked him, but her words whistled away on the wind. As she watched him disappear, she realised he'd never told her his name. She frowned. How rude. Crimson ducked inside the pub, resolving to put him from her mind and focus on her future.

---

[1] Crimson had read the sign correctly. It harked back to the time when a small hamlet called Gull's Bottom existed, less a village than a collection of fisherfolks' houses. It was so named for the white birds that flew overhead and was the source of many a cruel joke at the expense of the hardworking people who lived there until, in the way of things, the town of Woolton expanded and absorbed the village and its name. And here you thought the author was making a cheap joke.

Chapter 3

~ *The Drunken Gull* ~

As Crimson stamped her feet on the worn welcome mat, all chatter stopped. The minstrel in the corner twanged a mis-chord at her sudden entrance. Heads swivelled and the hard glare of eyes assessed the newcomer.

The sour smell of stale beer and rotting fish hung thick in the air. Crimson breathed through her mouth, pulled back her hood and gave her cheeriest smile. "Hello, pleased to meet you all. I'm new here and would love to know where I can find a shop that might be vacant…and available to rent…" She trailed off.

The patrons turned back and resumed their conversations.

Undeterred, Crimson headed for the bar where a tall cyclops wiped a glass with a rag. "Good afternoon to you, sir."

"Drink?"

"Er, a lemonade please," she squeaked. "And do you have any food?"

"This 'ere lady wants a lemonade," the bartender announced to the bar, his bloodshot eye creasing with mirth.

Raucous laughter sounded back from the tables. Now Crimson could see, she noticed that the patrons were older folk hunched over their mugs of ale. A petalborn sat in the corner, violet eyes regarding her over a large pewter tankard.

Crimson shifted on her toes and hugged her arms around her cold body, making herself smaller. "Perhaps some information, then?"

"Information's more expensive. 'Specially for outsiders." The bartender's stare hardened as he looked her up and down, summing her up and finding her wanting.

Crimson wavered, surer than ever that she shouldn't have come here. She'd thought this place would be better than Oasis, but it was worse, much worse. No one wanted her here, and she had nowhere else to go.

She forced her spine to straighten. "I see. I'll go then."

Feeling the eyes of everyone in the bar on her, she battled the door open and stepped out into the storm. Even the weather was against her.

Crimson collapsed against the lime-washed wall, huddling under the eaves where the guttering dripped large blobs of rain onto the paved street. She put her head in her hands. This was all one big mistake.

The door banged.

"If you're after a shop to rent, you need to speak to the clerk. He knows all the properties in the area." A melodic female voice cut through the storm.

"Th-thank you." Crimson looked up into the purple face of the petalborn who had watched her in the bar.

"You were brave to come here."

Crimson sniffed. She didn't feel brave.

"Why didn't you go to the Salt and Pickle? You must have walked straight past it."

That so and so! Her guide had led her here deliberately instead of taking her to somewhere that might have helped her. Anger boiled through her, heating her in the chill of the lashing rain. "I think I've been the victim of a practical joke."

"Not much of a joke."

"No," Crimson agreed. "I don't suppose you could point me in the direction of the clerk's offices?"

"I'll take you. I've got to get back anyway before Duncan decides to come out and look for me."

Crimson nodded, not knowing who Duncan was.

The petalborn set off at a brisk pace, her long legs avoiding the growing puddles and streams of water rushing down the main street with ease. Crimson splashed behind her guide, her cloak hung heavy at her shoulders, soaked through with rain and mud.

"That building over there is the town council. Hardy's the clerk." With that, the petalborn left, disappearing into the sleeting rain. A shout echoed over the street as an afterthought. "And welcome to Saffron Vale."

Chapter 4

~ *Rumpy-pumpy* ~

"HELLO?" CRIMSON LOOKED AROUND the office. A light burned on a desk in defiance of the dark sky and awful weather. An old coat lay on the desk, as dark as shadows behind a faded nameplate that read; Anders Hardy. Files and heavy books lined the walls and a ceremonial staff coated in gold leaf lay glinting in a display cabinet.

A small cough behind her made her jump. She turned back to see the old coat was, in fact, a person.

"Can I help you?" He rubbed his eyes and blinked up at her.

"Oh, sorry to disturb you…"

"No need to apologise. I was reviewing some statutes and appear to have dozed off." He flashed her a small smile. "But nobody comes to the council offices without needing something. How can I help?"

Crimson darted over to the desk and thrust out her hand. "Crimson Brouderer and I'm looking for a shop. It's for my dresses, you see, I was in Juniper Vale but now I'm here because your cloth is so gorgeous and so I thought I'd come straight to the source for inspiration and, do you have anything?"

"Hmm," the clerk said in the peculiar tone familiar to all administrators, "there is one spot on the high street. It'll cost you…" He pulled a ledger towards him and ran his finger down a list of entries. "One hundred golds a month."

"A hundred." Crimson's jaw dropped. That was all the money she had with her. "Perhaps I could take some credit?" She injected the same confidence into her voice that she heard her old mentor use any time he negotiated with the guild.

The clerk tilted his head and smiled. "Regretfully, we do not accept credit for newcomers, unless you have a letter of standing? From a bank perhaps?"

Crimson shook her head, her heart sinking. Her lower lip trembled. She had travelled all this way, endured the bumpy roads and total lack of suspension in the travelling library for nothing. Now she was far from home, far from her friends, alone and homeless. She blinked back the hot tears that welled up in her eyes. It would do her no good to cry.

"Is there nowhere else?" she whispered.

As the clerk opened his mouth to answer, a short man in an embroidered waistcoat tailored to his plump form stepped out from a room behind the clerk's desk.

"Where's the ink? I need to write a letter of complaint to the newspaper."

The clerk sighed and pushed a large inkwell across the desk. "Are you sure?"

"There is a difference between rumpy and pumpy, so why, when it's put together, should it have a hyphen? That crossword writer has gone too far."

His eyes lit on Crimson, and a broad smile crossed his face. "Who is this delectable creature in our council offices, Hardy?"

Hardy answered him. "Crimson Brouderer from Juniper Vale. She wants to open a dress shop."

"Does she now?" He approached her, his hooved feet trapping on the wooden floor. The satyr took her hand in his and pressed it to his lips, leaving a smear of wet saliva on the back of her hand. She took her hand away and wondered if she could wipe the wetness off on her cloak without calling attention to the motion.

"Jollivity Bowan, Maire of this fair vale, at your service. What do you think of rumpy-pumpy?"

"Er…" Crimson felt the blush creeping up her neck at the inappropriate question.

"Hyphenated or not hyphenated?"

"Oh! I couldn't say."

"Rumpy-pumpy is not hyphenated[2]." The maire's eyes twinkled. "But enough of crosswords. How did such a fair maid cross into our lands from so far away on such a dismal day?"

"I came with a travelling library. We set off just after Lantern Night, but they headed to another vale first and I couldn't wait to get here, so I walked the last few miles."

"Ah, I do love to spread the old book-cheeks myself, but those travelling libraries do twist and turn in their routes. It's a wonder you got here before the saffron collection."

Crimson leaned forward. "So, there are crocuses?"

The maire let out a raucous laugh that had echoes of a bleating goat and was far too indecent for a council office. "Of course there are. Why do you think this is called Saffron Vale, m'dear?"

"Where are they?"

"Well, they don't bloom until the autumn. These aren't your ordinary springtime croci, these are saffron croci."

"Crocuses," muttered the clerk.

"So," Bowan said, ignoring his administrator, "you're taking on the old carver's place, are you?"

"Actually, no. It's a little out of my price range."

A gleam came into the satyr's eye. "Then, m'dear, I have

---

[2] You will notice, dear reader, that it is in fact hyphenated. But Jollivity Bowan never let grammar or correct writing get in the way of a good complaint.

just the thing."

"Maire Bowan, I really don't–" Hardy stood, his chair scraping on the wooden floor.

The maire held up a hand to silence the clerk. "Nonsense. It's a bit of a fixer upper right on the end of the High Street, but if you'll handle the repairs – within planning code, of course – I'll let you have it for a bum a month."

Crimson took a step back. "A bum?"

"Bumbles. Gold coins. Because they're gold, like bumblebees." He tilted his head to one side. "Don't you call them that? What did you think I meant, you saucy thing?"

Her face reddened until it was the same colour as her name. "Of course."

"So, what do you say? Do we have a deal?"

"I'll take it."

"Excellent. Make a note of it, Hardy." The satyr rubbed his hands together. "Now, this calls for a drink. Do we have any of the apple whisky?"

"You finished it at the weekend."

"Of course I did. Couldn't let old widow Ambrosia drink alone, could I? Do we have anything else in?"

"Apple juice or elderflower cordial."

The maire pulled a face. "Forgive our poor hospitality. Hardy, get to the Wrinkled Apple at once and purchase us some whisky."

The clerk's shoulders fell as he stood.

"Really, there's no need on my account," Crimson said. "I think I'd like to see this shop and get settled in. I have spent months on the road, so it'll be nice to have somewhere to call home."

"Of course." Maire Bowan eyed the rain hammering against the glazed windows of the offices. "I have some, er, important maire work to do. You show her the place, Hardy, and bring me back a bottle of whisky on your way back." With that, the maire snatched up the inkwell and headed back to his offices muttering about inept crossword compilers.

"Well, Miss Brouderer, shall we go and see your new premises?"

A short walk through the rain, which was now so thick, Crimson struggled to see the other side of the street, and they stopped outside an old building on the very end of the High Street. One of its shutters hung wonkily from its hinges as if it couldn't be bothered to even fall to the ground. Broken shingles lay on the ground and mushrooms sprouted from damp patches under the windows.

Crimson peered around. "Where is the shop?"

Hardy pushed open the door to the dilapidated building. "This is it."

Chapter 5

~ A night alone ~

CRIMSON FOLLOWED THE CLERK inside, her heart sinking into her stomach. This was the place where she was going to build her hopes and dreams? It was awful.

The stench of mould filled her nose and moss of all colours grew around the windows, which, she noted, had a single pane of glass hanging between warped lead casings. A steady drip fell through a hole in the roof. Lightning flashed through the sky, illuminating the disrepair in a flash of harsh light.

She couldn't build her new life here. It was a putrid hole of decay. Crimson bit the inside of her cheek to stave off the tears. She had travelled across the queendom for a fresh start and there was nothing here for her.

Crimson stepped further into the room, keeping her back to

the clerk so he couldn't see her face. Her hand closed on her mother's reel of thread in her pocket. All this time, she had thought she'd had signs to come to Saffron Vale and strike out on her own when the reality was that she had no plan and knew no one.

Her former mentor's voice sounded loud in her head. *Before you do anything, before you make the first cut in the fabric, you must see what you want to do.*

For all his faults and lack of acceptance, he had been a good mentor and taught her everything she knew about dressmaking. He would take her back. If she asked. Crimson shuddered. Just the thought of crawling back to him, begging him for the chance to be an assistant in his shop, made her want to shrivel up in a corner. That was one thing she couldn't do.

She'd left to do something new, to show that Crimson Brouderer could make it as a dressmaker without Guilder Senda's stamp of approval, without his grudging support. The only way she would ever return to Juniper Vale was if she was a successful designer, and to do that, she needed space, somewhere to call her own.

"If you want to say no to the maire, I can tell him that you didn't want to stay." The clerk stood just inside the door, trying to make himself as small as possible so he didn't touch anything.

Crimson clutched the wooden reel of thread so hard that it dug into her palm, the pain clearing her mind. This shop wasn't perfect, but nothing was. It was a start. A fresh start.

She sniffed. Alright, a not so fresh start. But it was something. And that was what she needed. Besides, if she could transform this place into a decent shop then she could do anything.

Squaring her shoulders, she turned to face Hardy. "If this is the only place available on the High Street, I'll take it." She walked over to a large table and ran her finger through the thick layer of dust. Forcing optimism into her voice, she said, "It just needs a spring clean and a bit of fixing up."

The clerk looked around the room with a hint of disbelief around his eyes. Perhaps he thought she was mad.

"Can you recommend anyone?"

He straightened his back and closed his mouth while he thought, seemingly pleased to be helpful now her decision was made. "Yes, there's a local woodsman who undertakes repairs and doesn't overcharge."

"He sounds perfect. How can I contact him?"

"I'll send him over in the morning. Is there anything else I can do?"

"No, thank you."

The clerk turned to go, then whirled back. "If you would be more comfortable at the Salt and Pickle Inn, I'm sure they will have a room. And I can confirm that their stargazey pie is the best you'll find on the West coast."

Tempting. Crimson's hand went to the reassuring weight of her coin purse, hidden inside a pocket. She needed every copper for her business. A little discomfort for a short while was nothing in the longer term. She shook her head.

"No, thank you. I am sure I have everything I need here. I brought food with me, enough for tonight at least. You have been so kind."

"If you need anything, you can find me at the town council office." With that, Hardy executed a small bow and left the shop. The door banged shut, then flew open as a gust of wind caught it.

Crimson rushed to shut it, forcing the wood closed against the gale that roared outside. After she managed to get the clasp in place, she leaned against the wood and buried her face in her hands. "Oh, stitches. What have I done?"

She allowed herself five minutes of despair before she uncovered her face and looked around the place. Evening had fallen, sending deep shadows around the room punctuated only by the quick sparks of lightning that burned across the sky followed by rolling thunder as if the queendom itself laughed at her plans.

Well, it had been a string of coincidences that had led her to choose Saffron Vale and she wasn't going to give up at the first dropped stitch. This was a challenge, nothing more. And she relished a challenge. That was how she had mastered her craft, by striving to do better, by tackling the more ambitious patterns, by forcing herself to learn and practice and never settling. And that was what she'd do here.

Taking a deep breath, she focused on practicalities. Light. That was the first thing. She reached into her bag and pulled out the remains of her Lantern Night candle. It had burned through the night during the festival and that was meant to bring good luck, so perhaps it would bring her luck here, too.

With shaking hands, she found one of the firesticks she had thought to bring. She had expected to light fires on the open road, but the travelling library had all necessities covered, so she'd never used them.

Taking a breath, she struck the head against the rough surface of the box and a small green flame danced on the end of the thin wooden stick. It worked. She laughed. The flame sputtered and she touched it against the wick of the fat beeswax candle – only the best for Lantern Night.

Now lit, the candle gave her courage and shielding it with her hand, she walked around her new shop. Her new shop! How she'd longed to say those words. When she hadn't made it into the guild, this had seemed like an impossibility, yet here she stood; a shop owner.

Crimson did a little jig of happiness, that she stopped as soon as the candle flickered wildly. She needed that light.

Keeping away from the hole in the roof, where water streamed in and formed a puddle close to the door, she explored the rest of her shop.

There was a small display area with a large counter. A strange stain spread over it, but the wood was thick and long, perfect for measuring out fabric. She added a measuring stick to her mental list of things she needed to purchase.

Behind the counter were cupboards, many with doors fallen off and a few stray pottery jars left from the previous occupants. They might be good for storing haberdashery.

Crimson tried to stay optimistic as she toed a rotting piece of wood. She'd need to add racks for fabric, of course, but there was ample wall space for that.

A small door led to a kitchen area with a large fireplace. Crimson covered her nose as the stench of bird droppings filled her nostrils. A pigeon sat on the table and cooed at her. A strange scratching noise came from the chimney. So, she wouldn't light any fires today.

A pinkish-grey ceramic blob sat on the kitchen side. Crimson picked it up and stifled a scream. It was possibly a pig, maybe a duck, or perhaps a demon from the depths of the underworld modelled in warped clay. Who would choose to purchase such an eyesore?

Crimson shoved it into a cupboard and shut the door with finality so she wouldn't have to look on the eldritch creation.

Pulling her sopping cloak around her, she tried the stairs, clinging onto the banister for support in case they gave way under her weight. A slow creak stopped her halfway. It wasn't worth the risk. Crimson crept back downstairs with a sigh.

"Guess I'm sleeping downstairs tonight," she said to herself.

The pigeon cooed again in agreement. Crimson left the stinking kitchen and retreated to the front of the shop, where she took off her cloak and changed into a dry dress before making a nest with her remaining clothes behind the counter.

It would do.

She set her candle on the countertop, ate a small meal of a wholemeal roll complete with a hunk of cheese washed down with a glug of water from her canteen, and settled down to sleep as the wind and rain howled outside.

Just as she nodded off, a loud crash jerked her from sleep.

The shutter exploded inwards, forced from its hinges. A dark shape flew across the room. Crimson screamed. The candle sputtered out under the sudden onslaught of wild wind.

Chapter 6

~ A new friend ~

THE SHADOW SKITTERED OVER the counter and collided with a jar in one of the cupboards, sending up a cloud of dust.

Crimson scuttled out from behind the counter, bumping into a wall in the dark.

Light. She needed light.

Crimson felt along the smooth wooden countertop until her fingers connected with the candle. She tore it loose from the waxy pool that held it in place and dug in her bag for the firesticks.

The creature banged around in the cupboard, snorting its wrath. It must be huge. Maybe it was a bear, or one of those rogue unicorns. Crimson swallowed and struck the firestick, making a flame. She lit the candle and held it up.

Emboldened now that she could see, Crimson grabbed the first thing she could find – a pottery jar – and held it aloft. So armed, she edged back around the counter.

The creature had somehow got under her cloak and had its head stuck in a cupboard. It grunted and let out a mighty sneeze that sounded like a roar.

Using her foot, Crimson swept her cloak from the beast, clutching the jar like a weapon.

A small dragon coated in yellow powder whined and tried to free itself from the cupboard again, growling in frustration as its horns stuck on the shelf.

A dragon! Crimson took a step back. She'd never seen one in person before. They were the sort of beast one saw in a book or, rarely, flying through the sky, but never up close and personal.

It snorted again and lay down, turning large eyes towards her like a stray dog.

Crimson swallowed. It might be a strange creature with its scales and claws, but it was in distress, and she could help.

"Oh, you poor thing." Crimson knelt on the floor and laid down her jar. "I think I see the problem here; you need to turn your head. Can you do that?" she asked in soothing tones. Talking to animals worked, didn't it? It worked on dogs and cats, why not dragons? Crimson edged forwards on her knees, moving slowly. Dragons might have sharper teeth, but they were animals too.

The dragon whined again and repeated its manoeuvre.

Crimson stopped her approach and gathered her courage.

"Alright, I can help you, but you have to promise not to bite me."

The dragon huffed out a breath and lay down on the floor.

"I'll take that as a yes." She held her breath and placed her hands on either side of its scaly head. "On three; one, two, three." With that, she twisted and pulled, and the dragon was free.

Crimson released it and pushed herself backwards as the small creature – no bigger than a medium-sized dog – wiggled its neck, gave a yelp of joy at its new freedom, and spread its wings.

It hopped up onto the counter and surveyed the shop before jumping down and running around the small space. Crimson leaned to one side so she could see what it was doing.

It sniffed the corners and put its front feet up on the window ledge, flicking its forked tongue at the storm that still raged outside.

With another sneeze, it dashed back behind the counter.

"Oh no, I'm very sorry, but you can't stay here. You have to go. Go on, shoo." Crimson waved her hands at the dragon. How did one convince a dragon to leave?

It tilted its head to one side and then eyed her abandoned nest of clothes.

"That is my bed."

It tilted its head to the other side and stepped onto the nest.

"No! No. Look, if you're determined to stay, here, you can have this." Crimson took out her oldest skirt and laid it down as far away from her as she could.

The dragon sniffed it, sneezed again, sending yellow powder into the air.

"You poor thing, you're covered in dust. May I?"

The dragon made a gesture with its head then lay down. Crimson took that as a yes.

Crimson picked up the skirt and ran the cloth over the dragon's scales. It responded by rubbing itself against her hand and emitting a low rumbling purr.

The powder stuck to the fabric, revealing the dragon's midnight purple scales.

"You're beautiful, aren't you?"

Another purr, as if the dragon agreed.

"Would you like some food? I don't know what dragons eat, but I have some dried meat and fruit." Crimson dug around in her pack and held out a piece of jerky.

The dragon sniffed at it and plucked it from her hand, devouring it with one gulp before licking her fingers with its snake-like tongue.

Crimson giggled at the ticklish sensation and scratched the creature's neck. It rewarded her with more purrs rumbling low in its throat before it disturbed the dust and sneezed again. "You must have found a jar of saffron. Pity, I could have sold it."

The dragon gave a small snort, possibly of commiseration.

Crimson frowned at a patch of yellow on its forehead that wouldn't come off.

"I guess if you're staying the night, you should have a name. How about Smudge? For that patch of moon yellow on your face."

The dragon huffed, although whether in agreement or not, Crimson couldn't tell. Now that she had stopped rubbing it down, the dragon snagged the skirt with its pointed teeth and dragged it to the corner, where it curled up next to the cupboard it had tried so hard to escape.

"Fine, you stay over there, and I'll sleep over here. And tomorrow, you can go back wherever you came from."

The dragon made a noise in the back of its throat and lay its head down. Crimson watched it by the small light of the candle as it settled into the rhythmic breaths of slumber.

Confident it wouldn't maim her while it slept, Crimson headed to the window and pushed the shutters back in place. Shards of glass reflected flashes of lightning. The last pane of glass had smashed.

Another bolt of lightning lit up the sky. Crimson yelped. A pale figure stood illuminated in the opposite doorway. Who would be out in this storm? The next streak of lightning revealed an empty doorway. Crimson shivered and wrapped her arms around herself. Perhaps it was a ghost. And wasn't that all she needed to top off this nightmare of a day?

She abandoned the window, making sure the shutters and door were fastened, pulled her own pile of clothes over her and tried to go back to sleep.

A knocking woke her seconds later. The first thing she noticed as she blinked awake was the stench of bad eggs, followed by a loud wheezing huffing sound. The dragon had not stayed in its corner, and had instead wormed its way to her bed where it now lay curled in her arms like a hot water bottle, snoring happily and sending its awful breath into her face.

Crimson pushed herself up. The dragon rolled over and stayed asleep. She couldn't help but smile down at the little creature.

The second thing she noticed was the milky sunlight streaming through the open shutter. The storm had passed, and it was daytime. Hours, not seconds, had passed while she slumbered. She had survived.

The third thing, which, she supposed, was really the first as it had woken her, was the incessant banging on the roof.

Smoothing her skirt, she waded through the puddle, which was now a small lake stretching across the floor, and opened the door. It hit something on the other side, and she shoved.

"Hey! Are you trying to kill me?"

Chapter 7

~ *We are not egg people* ~

ABANDONING THE DOOR, CRIMSON headed for the shutterless window and leaned out through the broken glass. Peering up, she saw a ladder leaned against the shop and someone on the roof.

"Stop destroying my shop!"

"I should have known it was yours. Who else but a clueless outsider would rent this hole?"

"Hey!" With some dismay, Crimson realised that it was the same woodsman who had mocked her the day before.

He carried on hammering. A shingle fell to the ground.

"Stop! You're ruining it!"

"I'm not ruining it."

"What are you doing, then?"

"Fixing the roof."

"Well, stop!"

"You don't want the roof repaired?"

"I do…"

He ripped out another of the slate shingles.

"I said stop!"

The man sighed, climbed down the ladder and faced her, leaning on the rotten windowsill and forcing her back. "What do you want?"

Crimson's mouth went dry at his closeness. "Your name," she squeaked before recovering her composure and repeating herself in a more normal voice. Great. Now he would think she was even more of an idiot than he did yesterday.

He levelled a look at her. "I don't give my name to outsiders."

She sighed and looked away. Her rainbow-flecked eyes marked her out as a teg, and no one trusted a teg. The mantra had been drilled into her by her former mentor. "I'm not trying to trick you, and I'm not an outsider anymore. See, I own this shop. I'm part of the town now."

"It takes more than renting a tumble-down shack to become part of this community. You can't just buy your way in, Red."

"My name is Crimson."

He shrugged and folded his arms.

Crimson sighed and repeated the mantra her old guild mistress had given her when dealing with awkward customers; you catch more bees with honey than with sour grapes.

"Look, if we're going to work together on this, let me at least buy you breakfast." She smiled.

He nodded.

"So, what would you like?"

"Ask for my usual."

"I need to know your name to get your usual." Her smile broadened.

His lips quirked up at one corner. "Mushroom omelette and a coffee. And go to Hambrosia for the omelette."

"OK, got it. Now, can you move your ladder so I can get outside?"

The handyman eyed her, but he stalked off and moved the ladder, even giving her a mock bow as she left the shop. A purple blur darted out behind her.

"Why do you have a dragon?"

Crimson took some satisfaction in seeing his jaw drop. "Oh, that's Smudge. He turned up last night." She tilted her head to the side as Smudge sniffed her skirts and sat down next to her, tongue lolling out of his snout. "I think he's decided to stay."

"How do you know it's a he?"

"I suppose I don't."

At that moment, the dragon relieved himself against the wall of the shop.

"Definitely a boy dragon."

Crimson didn't know where to look or what to say, so she ignored the man's comment. "Come on, Smudge, let's get some breakfast."

In the early morning daylight, the town had a charm that the rain had hidden last night. The buildings were less planned than in Oasis, leaning against one another as if they held each other up against the brisk wind. But they were quaint in a higgledy-piggledy way, and all topped with shining slate shingles that morphed from deep grey to an inky blue under the rising sun.

It was a shame the buildings themselves were so drab. No imagination had gone into any of the external décor; even the shop signs were simple lettering and an outline picture, nothing elaborate. As she daydreamed about the perfect sign for her own shop, a mouth-watering smell surrounded her.

Bacon.

She followed the aroma across the street, smiling as people moved to one side to let her and Smudge pass. A couple gaped at the dragon at her feet, and hurried past. Crimson kept the smile fixed on her face as she traced the divine bacon scent to a shop called Hambrosia and stared. Bacon and ham and every sort of pig product hung in the window, but nothing else. At her side, Smudge snuffled, drool dripping from the corner of his jaw.

Crimson stepped inside. A small fire burned in the hearth at one end and the smell of herbs mixed with frying bacon in an irresistible combination as it floated over the neatly set tables and chairs.

"Can I help you, Miss?" A youthful orc with the most glorious green skin – the colour of a spring birch leaf – stood behind a counter which displayed bacon scones and even a chocolate cake topped with candied bacon. "Is that a dragon? Chill. I've only seen them swimming in the sea! How did you get one as a pet? What does it eat?"

"I have no idea."

The boy plated up some burned bacon bits from a jar on the counter and placed it on the floor. Smudge sniffed the plate and licked it clean.

"I think he's a fan." Crimson smiled. "Can I have some bacon for the dragon, two coffees, a bacon sandwich and a mushroom omelette, please?"

"What?" A large orcish woman burst out from behind a set of swinging doors. She loomed over Crimson. "What did you say?"

"I just placed an order…" Crimson looked to the younger man for help, and he gave her the sort of eyeroll that all teenagers give at their parents' behaviour.

"You asked for an…an…omelette!" The woman spat the word, her greenish skin darkening in her anger.

"Do you not sell them here, only–"

"What kind of simpleton are you? We do not sell egg products here! Everyone knows that!"

"I'm new to town and–"

The woman puffed up, no doubt intending to launch into a

rant about newcomers, but this time her son intervened. "It's chill, Mum. I'll deal with her order and show her where she can get an omelette."

"Do not speak that word in my presence, Hamlet! And don't you dare go into that…place." She said the word with such venom that Crimson took a step back.

"A bacon sandwich, please, Mum."

Huffing about 'no good eggs', the orc stomped back into the kitchen.

"What was all that about?" Crimson whispered.

The young orc shook his head and poured her coffees. "White or black?

"What milk do you have?"

The teenager behind the counter pulled a confused face. "Cow."

"And?"

"And we can maybe get sheep's milk…"

Crimson covered her disappointment at the lack of nut milk with a smile. "Cow's milk then, please." She paused and realised she had no idea how the handyman took his coffee. "And put one milk in a separate cup please, and sugar in another."

He crinkled his brow but made up her order and handed her a small tray with four ceramic cups on it. "Return them for two coppers off on your next purchase," the orc said.

Moments later, two packages wrapped in greaseproof brown

paper and tied with string appeared in the window to the kitchen accompanied by a hollered "Order up!"

The teenager handed them to Crimson, who balanced the tray in one hand and the packages in another, trying to stop her mouth watering from the tempting smell of cooked bacon as she followed him outside.

He strutted across the street, passing a rock tied to a piece of string hanging from a sign that proclaimed it was a weather-stone.

"Is that like weatherweed?" Crimson asked, referring to the seaweed that changed depending on the rain.

"Sort of."

Crimson looked up at the sign and read the description:

If I be wet, it be raining.
If I be dry, it be not.
If I be swaying, it be windy.
If ye cannot see me, it be fog.
If I be gone, it be a hurricane.

"Well, that's ridiculous." What was this backwater town if it relied on a rock to tell them the weather? You might as well look out of the window.

Hamlet shrugged and led them on to a shop almost opposite Hambrosia called Eggselcior. This shop's window display showed eggs of every shape, size and colour arranged into flowers.

A teenage dwarf moved a cloth across the countertop in a lacklustre motion while gazing at the wall with a bored expression until the boy coughed. Then she looked up, smiled and blushed before rushing over to the door with a furtive look over her shoulder.

"What are you doing here?"

"Forty thousand men could not keep me from your side, fair Ovelia."

"Maybe so, but my Dad will have your guts for garters if he finds you in our shop."

"Then I shall wait just outside until the day we can be together." Hamlet pressed his lips to the back of the girl's hand, and she blushed again.

A scraping noise came from the back of the shop and Hamlet blanched and took a step back. So, he wasn't as cocky as he appeared, thought Crimson.

He coughed and gestured to Crimson. "This is a newcomer to town. She asked for an omelette."

Ovelia stared at Crimson. "At Hambrosia?"

Crimson nodded.

The girl burst out laughing. "How did your mum take it?"

"She didn't throw anything," Hamlet said, vying for Ovelia's attention.

"That's progress."

A loud bang accompanied by a grunt rang out across the

shop.

"We shall yet be together, my sweet." Eyeing the door to the backroom, Hamlet kissed Ovelia's hand again and backed away down the street.

Ovelia watched him go with a dopey smile on her face. Young love. Crimson's lips tightened as an image of her first crush came unbidden into her mind. Her hand clenched around the packet of bacon, squashing the spongy bread down. Another thing her former friend had ruined.

"So, you wanted an omelette?"

Crimson nodded and rearranged the packages in her hands so she didn't destroy her breakfast. "With mushrooms, please. He said it was his usual."

A small frown crinkled the girl's brow before she smiled. "You must mean Lief. He's the only one who's got a usual with mushrooms. Is that a dragon? I've never seen one as a pet before."

Lief was it? Crimson's smile turned into one of self-satisfaction. She had his name.

"Yes. His name's Smudge, he's decided to stay." The small dragon sat by Crimson's feet, drool dripping from his jaws onto the floor in an ever-growing puddle.

The dwarf snorted. "I think he wants some food."

Crimson unwrapped the bacon and held out her hand. The dragon snatched the meat out of her hand and Crimson laughed with relief that she still had all her fingers. They would have to work out a better way of feeding him.

A brawny dwarf burst into the room, his nose up in the air like he was tracking something. "You alright, Ovelia?"

"Fine, Dad. Just serving a customer."

The dwarf opened his mouth. And closed it again. "Is that a dragon?"

"Er, yes."

He shook his head. "A pet dragon, well I never." Another shake of his head and the dwarf dragged his gaze from the reptile back to his daughter. "I thought I could smell bacon."

"This lady brought some in."

He sniffed, then huffed out the air as if the bacon had offended him. "That's alright then. I thought it was that Hamlet boy back again. No good troublemaker."

"Da-ad," Ovelia's voice had the unique quality of all teenage voices that conveyed the maximum annoyance and embarrassment with the minimum of syllables.

"He is. That whole family ought to be thrown out of town. Good for nothing pig orcs." The dwarf tugged on his beard and hawked up a gobbet of phlegm. He looked around for somewhere to spit, realised there was only the floor of his shop so swallowed his phlegm, before glaring out at the shop almost across the street.

"He's not his mum," Ovelia said, but quietly.

"That whole family is trouble. Ever since old Tricky Hamble tricked–"

"–Great Grandmother out of her chicken farm. I know, Dad. Back in the mists of time when the great lobster spoke to the people daily and gods roamed the land." Ovelia rolled her eyes. Crimson hid her smile. This sounded like an exchange that had happened many times before.

"Yes, well. Stay away from him." With that, the dwarf disappeared through the swinging doors.

Another eye roll, then Ovelia chopped up some mushrooms and fried them in thick creamy butter, jostling the fungi with a wooden spatula as if they'd offended her.

"So, you're not meant to be friends with Hamlet…" Crimson leaned against the counter, unable to help herself. She had to know the story here.

Ovelia sighed as she buttered another pan. "It's complicated." She cracked the eggs, and loud sizzling filled the shop for a few moments, making it impossible to talk. "You know how it is. Two merchant families both alike in dignity and pride from ancient grudge do take it out on their children."

There had been rivalries back in Oasis, but nothing so deep that children were forbidden to talk to each other.

With a deft flick of her wrist, Ovelia added the mushrooms to the omelette, followed by a spoonful of chopped, dried herbs that filled the shop with the scent of garlic and freshness as the omelette finished cooking. She packed it up into a flimsy box with a sad smile and Crimson's heart panged for the star-crossed lovers. There must be something she could do.

She said as much to the heartsick teenager, who shrugged in

return. "Best to leave it alone. This thing between our families is generations old. It won't be solved so simply." And Ovelia began scrubbing down the grill with a metal brush.

Crimson had a lot to think about on the walk back to her shop.

Chapter 8

~ I know how to work hard ~

SHE FROWNED IN ANNOYANCE at the ladder still blocking her doorway. Hammering sounded from somewhere on the roof.

"Excuse me. Excuse me!" she called up, trying to ignore the passersby, who stared at the strange woman shouting in the street.

"Yes?" Lief's face appeared with an annoying, cheerful smile on it. His gaze landed on the packages Crimson carried. "Did you find breakfast?"

"Come down so I can move this ladder and get inside."

"Alright, calm down, Red. I'm coming." He took his time climbing down and wiping his hands on his thick work trousers.

Crimson noted the worn areas, faded and threadbare around

his knees. She could offer to patch them. Then she remembered. "You asked me to get you an omelette from Hambrosia."

His lips quirked up on one side and his eyes widened in innocence. "Did I?"

"Except, everybody knows, well everybody except me, that they don't sell eggs at Hambrosia."

"No? What did Greezi say?"

"Oh, the orc? She politely explained my mistake and pointed me to Eggselsior, where I got you this." Crimson shoved the omelette at him.

Disappointment flashed across his face. "Really?"

"The polite thing to say would be, thank you," she paused, "Lief."

He leaned against her house and unwrapped the packet. "So, you found out then."

"Yes." Crimson couldn't help the self-satisfaction that bubbled off her in waves. She had won a point in this strange town. It felt like her luck was changing after that terrible first night.

"Hmm."

She had expected a stronger reaction than that, but it would do. "Now, if you'll excuse me, I want to get inside and find a plate."

He gave her an amused look, but stepped aside and tilted the ladder so she could get in. Ugh, that man was so annoying. He didn't even have the common courtesy to say thank you.

Crimson strode into the kitchen and stopped. In her anger, she had forgotten that it was uninhabitable. That strange scratching sound in the chimney was back, and the dragon growled from where he crouched at her feet.

"Let's find a plate, Smudge." Her voice was too cheerful, even to her own ears. She placed her sandwich and the drinks on a side, opened a cupboard with her fingertips and stepped back, expecting something to leap out at her. When nothing did, she bent down to look and grinned. Plates in the first cupboard. Perfect. Smudge lay lower against the floor and huffed.

She pulled one out, sending unknown tiny insects scurrying away from her. With a shudder, she kicked the door shut and studied her prize. It was a plain plate coated with a rough glaze that may have been an earthy reddish orange under the thick layer of dust.

Crimson's gaze caught on the hand pump above a ceramic sink. Indoor plumbing! A luxury she hadn't had in Oasis. She grabbed the pump. It wouldn't budge.

"Stitches!" she swore. She took the handle with both hands and heaved, forcing the rusty metal down. It groaned in protest and then a sludgy black substance sputtered from the tap onto the plate. Crimson screamed in surprise, then gagged at the stench of stale water and scummy slime and fled the kitchen.

She collided with Lief racing through the main room. "Oof."

"What happened? I heard a scream." He gripped her arms tight enough to hurt.

Crimson shook him off. "I am quite alright. The tap shocked me."

He lifted an eyebrow. "I thought it was only the maire's house that had indoor plumbing." He brushed past her into the kitchen. Two seconds later, he was back at her side, his hand over his mouth.

"That is foul. It's worse than Bowan after he's been in the bins."

"The maire?"

Lief shrugged. "He's a satyr. Not his fault he's half goat. Keeps the paperwork down and people in politics have worse vices." He aimed a thumb at the kitchen. "You'll have to sort that out."

Crimson pulled herself away from the image of the maire eating rubbish. She drew herself up to her full height, coming up to Lief's chest. "That is exactly what I plan to do, as soon as I've finished my breakfast."

She stomped back into the kitchen, holding her breath against the stench, and retrieved her sandwich and the drinks.

"I got this for you, too. I didn't know how you take it, so there's milk in the smaller cup. They only had cow's milk."

"What other sort of milk is there? Sheep?"

"Nut."

Lief screwed up his face. Crimson narrowed her eyes at his confusion. Was he having her on again?

"You know; nut milk. Almond, pistachio, hazelnut. Or oat milk."

"How do oats make milk?"

Crimson opened her mouth, then closed it again as she considered. "You know, I really have no idea. But it's real." She folded her arms. "Makes a delicious latte."

"I'll take your word for that."

They sipped their drinks in silence, reaching some sort of understanding or perhaps grudging acceptance. Crimson wasn't sure what exactly they understood, but it was better than arguing.

Lief looked around the interior with a sceptical gaze. "You know this is going to take a lot of work to get anywhere close to being habitable."

Crimson sighed. "I know, but the maire was so kind to give me a bargain."

"Bargain?" he snorted. "He's got the better end of the stick if you're paying him for this place."

"It's a prime shop front. Or it will be once I've cleaned it up."

"You're going to clean it up." Disbelief laced his voice.

Crimson bristled. "Yes, me. Who else?"

"You just don't look like the type to get your hands dirty."

"What do you know about my hands Mr won't-even-tell-people-his-name?"

He grabbed her hand and pulled it close to his face, running his thumb over her palm. His hot breath grazed her skin and Crimson swallowed as nervous heat pooled in her stomach.

Lief peered at her palm with an expression she couldn't place before he changed, almost shuttered down in front of her. He grinned, wearing it like a mask, and released her.

"No callouses on your palms. Never done a day's work in your life."

Crimson lifted one eyebrow and smiled as she retrieved a pin from her pocket. Her mouth curved into a smile. She took the pin and stabbed it into the pad of her index finger where her skin had hardened from years of hard work.

He started forward, and she did it again, stopping him in his tracks.

"I might not have the same callouses as someone who lives in the forest and repairs roofs, but I'm a trained tailor and dressmaker and these hands have seen more work than you can imagine. My fingers are needle proof from all the years of sewing I've done, and that is how I earn my living."

"You're mad."

Crimson inclined her head, acknowledging the room they stood in. "Perhaps. But I will succeed because I know how to work hard and, despite what you might think, I'm not afraid of getting my hands dirty."

"Well, well, the kitten has claws. You might pull this off after all, Red. It'll take some time, though."

"As I don't have any stock to sell, time is not a problem. For now, anyway."

He didn't press her on what that meant, and she was grateful. It was becoming painfully apparent to her that her plan had more holes in it than a moth-eaten dress. But, as with mending fabric, she would focus on one thing at a time.

Crimson looked away from his sharp gaze. "I need your help though," she said through gritted teeth, hating having to ask this arrogant man for anything.

"Oh?"

"I need rags for cleaning, and an apron. I didn't think to bring…anything like that."

"You didn't think you'd need cleaning products?" he asked.

Stitches. She should have bought some while she was in town. But that was the problem; she focused on the problem in front of her and this morning, flustered by the large man outside her house, she had fixated on breakfast instead of supplies.

In her mind, Crimson went through everything she had with her; one change of clothes, a small amount of travelling rations left, her money and her cloak. Smudge nuzzled against the back of her legs. And a dragon.

Nothing spare she could cut up and clean with. No idea where to start sourcing her cloth and, until the shop was clear, nowhere to work.

"Never mind. I'll sort it." She tramped out of the shop, leaving Lief standing there.

"Don't forget your purse," he called after her.

"It's in my pocket," Crimson shouted back.

"What is a pocket?"

Crimson span on her heels and looked Lief in the eye. "Are you mocking me?" His blank look cooled her anger and she showed him the slit in her dress where her pocket hung, perfect for carrying her purse without needing a bag.

"Well, aren't you full of surprises, Red."

"My name is Crimson!" With that, she stormed off.

Chapter 9

~ A discovery of chocolate ~

CRIMSON REALISED HER MISTAKE halfway down the street. She had stormed off with no idea where to go, and now she couldn't turn around in case Lief saw her uncertainty. He was a bully. A bully who hated people, or at least outsiders like her. One of those ignorant country types who didn't take kindly to new ideas. Not unlike her former mentor who had scuppered her chance at joining the guild because her ideas were too radical, too fresh for the traditional guilders.

She forced herself to take a breath. It had been months, but the wound of rejection, betrayal and torn dreams was still raw in her heart.

A wonderful smell wafted down the road, turning her head. Chocolate.

"Come on, Smudge."

Crimson followed her nose, ignoring the stares of townsfolk as she passed and grateful she wore her more muted travelling dress. Her other one was much brighter and had contrasting pockets, which seemed to be a new innovation in Saffron Vale if Lief's reaction was anything to go by.

As the delicious chocolate scent bloomed, she saw the shop and hurried to the window. A painted sign advertised the café as The Cozy Lobster and the curved window showed people sat at tables with morning drinks. Not just a chocolate shop, but a café as well. With a sigh of happiness, she went inside.

A cheerful woman with curved horns twisting back over her purple tendrils of hair smiled from behind the counter.

"Be with you in a minute," she said.

Crimson nodded and stepped up to the counter. There was one of the ingenious machines that turned water and coffee beans into a wonderful elixir, and the rich smell of chocolate mixed with the bitter coffee in a heady aroma that reminded Crimson of the coffee shops at home. At Oasis, she corrected herself. This place was her home now, and the sooner she remembered that, the better.

On the counter, behind a glass pane, sat rows of cakes and tiny chocolates that promised mouth-watering flavours.

"Is that a dragon? Is it yours?"

"This is Smudge. He's staying with me for now."

"Wow, I don't think I've ever seen a dragon as a pet. Does he like chocolate?"

"No idea. He loves bacon, though."

The woman smiled and bent to offer Smudge a chocolate drop.

"Careful, he's not trained." The last thing Crimson needed was for her nominal pet dragon to hurt someone. That would be the worst way to earn her place among these people.

But Smudge was on his best behaviour. He flicked his tongue out and delicately took the proffered chocolate without leaving so much as a smear of dribble on the woman's hand. Perhaps she should make him a harness, maybe in violet to match his scales.

"There, he likes it." The lady beamed, showing pointed teeth and a forked tongue of her own. "Now, what can I get you?"

"Are you really a member of the Tasters' Guild?" Crimson gestured to the badges that lined the wall behind the counter. She recognised the crest of the Tasters' Guild who aimed to create the most perfect Heart of the Vale chocolate drink, and underneath that there was the grinder and beans of the Coffee Makers' Guild and the herbs of the Worshipful Tea Masters as well as one she didn't recognise with a lobster etched into it.

"I am." The woman's chest swelled with pride. Crimson didn't blame her. It was a big achievement to get into one guild, let alone four.

"That's amazing."

"Although that one is really a shopkeeper's association here in Woolton, but still, not everyone gets accepted."

"I should look into that, I suppose."

"Opening a new shop, are you?"

Crimson nodded. "A dressmaker's, not for a while though." She sighed as she thought about everything there was to do.

"You should speak to Dilly; she's an upstanding member of the association."

"Great. Where can I find her?"

"Right here." Dilly smiled as Crimson looked around before she realised that the café owner was referring to herself.

"Pleased to meet you, I'm Crimson Brouderer, dressmaker and tailor."

"Lovely. And what would you like to drink?"

Crimson ordered a hot chocolate and some water for Smudge and asked the price of the spheres of chocolate coated with almonds and sugar. She blinked at the amount charged. She should have known that if the price wasn't printed clearly, then it was too expensive. Chocolate making was an art, but it was one she couldn't afford unless she wanted to end up homeless. Her mouth watered. Maybe it would be worth it for a little taste.

She almost gave in before her resolve hardened. She could go without until she was a successful businesswoman who could afford chocolate and Heart of the Vale drinks every day. Crimson sighed at the pleasant daydream as she found a seat near the fire and hung her cloak to dry on the back of her chair. Steam curled from its fabric as it finally had a chance to dry after the storm.

Dilly brought over the hot chocolate with a small square of

dark chocolate set on the saucer and a plate containing a huge golden scone snuggled in between a pot of strawberry jam and another containing the thickest cream Crimson had ever seen.

"Oh, no, I haven't paid–"

"This," Dilly put down the scone, "is to welcome you to the vale. And this," she pointed to the chocolate, "is something new I'm working on. I need customer feedback. In fact, if you promise to be honest with me, I'll happily bring you something every time you come in."

"Deal." Crimson popped the square in her mouth and closed her eyes as the chocolate melted on her tongue. It was smooth and creamy and, she opened her eyes, spicy. Crimson coughed and Dilly brought her a glass of water.

"Too hot?"

"What was that?" asked Crimson when she could speak. Her tongue still felt swollen.

"I mixed in some peppercorn and chillies; it tasted good to me."

"Maybe it's just me. I'm not used to spice."

Dilly shook her head. "No, it's not you. I've had this reaction from everyone, but I'll keep working on it. Here," she handed her a shot glass filled with milk, "this will cleanse your palette before you have your hot chocolate."

Crimson downed the milk and turned her attention to the fluffy scone. She dipped a knife into the cream. The bustle of the café fell silent. All eyes turned to her.

"What's going on?" she asked out of the corner of her

mouth.

Dilly leaned over and took the knife out of the cream. The hubbub of café conversation resumed, rising until it resembled the hum of a contented beehive, if bees also clinked their cups against saucers as they discussed the day's catch.

"Best to put the jam on first in this vale."

"Really?" That there could be an incorrect order to jam and cream on baked goods had never occurred to Crimson.

"If you don't want to offend anyone."

"Jam first it is." Crimson dolloped a blob of rich red jam onto her scone, and, after a nod from Dilly, followed that with a generous portion of clotted cream. She needed to win people over, not make enemies because she put condiments on her scones in the wrong order.

Dilly took a seat, folding her left leg over her right and leaning back. "So, what brings you to Saffron Vale?"

Crimson sipped her drink, enjoying the rich creamy taste of hot chocolate before she answered. She decided not to go into the betrayal by her best friend or how her mentor had ripped out her dreams and instead gave the simplest answer. "I found this material and wanted to come to the source."

She pulled out the swatch of bright yellow fabric that had first piqued her interest in this vale and that she kept with her as some sort of good luck talisman, or a reminder that her future was bright, or a fool's hope that being close to the type of people that made these vibrant colours would mean they were open to her ideas.

So far, she hadn't seen much of that. Everyone she had met wore simple clothing in faded colours and even the houses were grey.

She handed the fabric to Dilly, who rubbed it between her fingers before handing it back as if it wasn't the source of all Crimson's hopes for this place.

"Well, there's certainly plenty of dyers round here and the best saffron in the queendom. Hardy will have the sourcebook if you want to check."

"Sourcebook?"

Dilly nodded. "Every dyer that's selling cloth in the vale sends a patch to the town council so it can be logged according to colour and quality. It prevents arguments and allows families to protect their recipes. Anything else I can do for you?"

"Er, I don't suppose you have any rags or cleaning things I could borrow?"

Dilly's eyebrow raised and her slitted pupils widened.

"Only the place I've rented is a bit of a fixer-upper. It's at the end of the High Street."

"The old sweet shop?" That explained the stain on her counter, sugar and colouring were a nightmare to get out of fabric, so it stood to reason that it would be tough to get out of wood too. "I thought that was condemned for demolition."

Crimson bit her lip. She would not cry.

"But I'm sure it's fine. Of course, I'll drop some supplies up after the morning rush. Speaking of, better dash." With that,

Dilly pushed herself up. "And I'm guessing you haven't any dinner plans. Go to the bakers at the end of the day and he'll have something for you." With that, she made her way back to the counter to continue serving.

Crimson took her time over the luxurious hot chocolate, savouring the drink as the rare treat it would have to be until she could turn her fortunes around, and then headed over to the town council, gripping the small fabric swatch like a lifeline.

Chapter 10

~ *Ignatius Copplebottom* ~

"M ISS BROUDERER," HARDY STOOD, unfolding himself from behind his desk, and greeting her warmly. "How was your first night at your new place?"

"A little eventful, but now I have Smudge, who's decided to stay with me for a while."

Hardy eyed the small dragon. "Is it house trained? We have a lot of papers here…"

"I'm sure he'll behave himself, won't you, Smudge?"

The dragon huffed and Crimson tensed, half expecting him to breathe out flames and set the building alight. Her shoulders sagged with relief when Smudge took himself off and curled up in a corner.

"So, how can I help? If you want to get out of your contract with the maire, I'm sure he'll be more than reasonable."

"No, nothing of the sort. This is the only way I can afford a place on the High Street and the roof's nearly fixed," Crimson said, hoping that was true and that Lief could fix the roof today. "I'd like to know who made this cloth, or rather, who dyed it."

She handed over the fabric to the clerk, who squinted as he studied it, twisting the fabric to and fro as he tested the tensile strength.

"Well, that shouldn't be a problem, if you're sure if came from our vale?"

"Yes." She had bought it from Bright back in Oasis and the kobold never lied about her stock.

Hardy took an enormous book from the shelf and opened it to reveal pages of pockets. Each one had spidery letters and numbers scrawled across it.

"These tell me the brightness, who manufactured it, type of cloth used and fastness of colour," Hardy explained as he caught her staring. "This book contains all the yellow colours from mustard to primrose, so I think we'll find it…"

So many yellows. Crimson loved colour. Finding the perfect combination made her heart sing and her needle fly with happiness as she created, but even she had never imagined so many shades of just one colour.

"Now, this is bright, so it will be at this end of the yellow spectrum and sturdy cloth with a neat, tight weave. How about this?" Hardy pulled out a small square of material. "No, not quite right…"

He continued in this fashion for some time until the clerk let out a small "Aha!" and showed Crimson the matching fabric for her to compare.

She took both pieces to the window for better light. They were identical.

"Yes," she breathed, "please tell me who made this wonderful cloth."

Crimson handed back the sample swatch and waited as Hardy reviewed the codes. He peered up at her with a strange, almost apologetic look on his face. "That fabric and dye was created by Ignatius Copplebottom."

Chapter 11

~ *Complex thinking* ~

CRIMSON STOOD OUTSIDE THE smooth lighthouse, twisting her skirts in her hand. This was it. The place where the brightest colour she had seen had been created. The fabric that had inspired her to come to this Vale above all others.

Leaving Smudge to chase bugs in the long grass that lapped at the base of the tower, she climbed up the ladder and knocked on the door set a few feet off the ground, taking in the dark iron key holes of every shape and size that appeared in the wood in odd places. Was that one by a hinge?

Silence.

This time, she hammered on the wood with her fist as uncertainty swirled through her mind. What if this Ignatius Copplebottom wasn't at home? What if he hated people? That certainly seemed to be a feature of some of Saffron Vale's residents. An image of Lief flashed through her head, accompanied by a burst of anger. How much had Hardy promised him for working on her house, anyway?

She added 'check price of handyman' to her mental to-do list.

A voice interrupted her brooding. "Come in, it's not locked."

Crimson eyed the many key holes and tried the handle. The door swung open on well-oiled hinges and Crimson's jaw dropped.

Inside the house were…things. Complicated machinery lay in bits on every surface, something with wings hung from the ceiling and notes papered the walls, some written on the peeling plaster itself. Stairs hugged the outside wall leading up to more rooms and, presumably, the light at the very top. A stack of certificates lay on a table, marked with rings of stale tea. By the table, a rocking chair sat stationary with something that looked like a torture device formed of threads and sticks above it. As she took in the shambolic surroundings, she became aware of a dull whistle.

"Over here! Quickly, if you please!" An arm coated in tawny brown feathers waved frantically from behind a wooden screen. It took Crimson a moment to register that the feathers were not part of an elaborate outfit but were because the speaker was a tylluan – an owl-like entity common in the vales. It took another moment for her to realise that the dull whistle had become shriller and more urgent.

Crimson ran over to where the arm waved and crouched behind the screen.

"I'm Crimson–" she started.

The arm waver cut her off with another gesture and peeked over the top of the screen where the whistling had grown to a crescendo. "Any second now..." He beamed through enormous goggles that magnified his eyes to terrifying proportions above his jet-black beak.

"What's happening?" Crimson shouted over the din.

"Well, you see," said the owl man, his voice rising as the whistling continued to wail around the room, "in actual fact, we appear to have made TEA!" He shouted the last word just as the whistling stopped. "Ah, yes. Tea. Would you like a cup?" He asked the question with such hopefulness that Crimson nodded, painting a smile on her face.

The man rubbed his hands together, the small feathers on top of his head stiffening in excitement. "Excellent! Then let us have a look."

He strode out from behind the screen and over to a small kettle now pouring hot, brown water into a single mug, which he handed to Crimson.

"Aren't you having any?"

"Me? Oh, it only makes one cup. This is the first successful pour."

Something made Crimson look up. A kettle hung embedded in one of the wooden beams that laced the ceiling.

"Go on, try it." He leaned forward and Crimson studied the

drink.

It looked like tea, if over-brewed. She sniffed. It smelled like some sort of herbal tea. She blew on the drink and took a sip before pulling a face.

"Oh dear," he said.

"It's not so bad," she said, "a little…strong for my liking."

"Yes," he sighed, "I thought that might happen."

He walked over to a standard kettle hung over a fire and poured two cups in the regular manner. "It's about the brewing, you see. I'm certain of it. There must be a faster way."

"To make tea?"

"Precisely! If we can apply complex thinking to something as simple as making tea, think what else we might achieve." He lifted his goggles, revealing large amber eyes. "It's so nice to meet a fellow experimenter. Have we met before?" He blinked at her.

"Oh, I'm not an experimenter, per se. I wanted to see you about this." Crimson pulled the piece of fabric from her pocket.

"Ah yes." He took it from her and nibbled it with his beak before handing it back. "It's a piece of cloth."

"I know that!"

"Oh." But his attention had wandered back to the tea machine. "I wonder if I de-pressurised the tea leaves…perhaps that would counteract the high concentration of the steam." He took out a notebook and started scribbling.

Crimson stepped forward again. "Mr Copplebottom–"

"Ig."

"Sorry?"

"Call me Ig. Mr Copplebottom sounds so formal, and Ignatius is hardly any better and my middle name is Benedict. Makes you wonder what my parents were thinking. Ig is what my friends call me, and we shared tea." He nodded as if working through an internal script. "Friends share tea and therefore we must be friends. It's simple logic."

"Yes, of course," Crimson said. "I wonder if I might have your attention for a moment. Hardy informed me that you dyed this fabric."

"Did he now? How marvellous! Then I expect I did. Let me see it again." He snatched the fabric back and held it up in the dim light. "Tosh."

"Then you didn't dye it?"

"What? Oh, yes, I did. Last year. But it's rubbish. It'll fade after a mere three hundred washes."

"But that's brilliant." Crimson pulled herself up. "Mr, I mean, Ig, I would like to buy some of your fabric."

"Oh, I don't make that colour any more."

Crimson sagged.

"I've got something much better, much brighter."

Crimson dared to hope again. Something brighter than the most vibrant yellow she had ever handled. This was why she had chosen Saffron Vale.

"Do you want to see?" The tylluan looked up at her with that innocent hope again that someone might be interested in his work.

"Yes, I would love to see your new fabric."

"Excellent. Then let us away to the river."

Chapter 12

~ *The rainbow river* ~

I G GRABBED A SATCHEL and climbed out of the house.

"Don't you want to lock the door?" Crimson asked as she followed him down to the ground.

"Whatever for?"

"You have all those locks."

"Oh, those." Ig let out a hooting laugh. "I was experimenting with locking mechanisms for a commission and had to lock something. It's fascinating, really. Did you know that anything can be a key if you have the right lock? I say, is that a dragon? Fascinating. What happened to its wing?"

"He crashed into my shop last night. I tried to bandage it."

"May I?"

Crimson nodded, and Ig bent down and unwrapped the makeshift bandage.

"Hmm, not broken," he said, moving the delicate wing between his fingers. "But sprained. I have something that may help. Wait here!"

With that, he climbed back into his lighthouse and loud crashes sounded for a few moments before he returned, gliding down from the high door with ease.

Crimson stroked Smudge's head, licking her finger to try to remove the mark on his forehead while they waited for the tylluan to land.

He waved a small pot of something with a flourish and opened it.

Crimson took a step back as the stench of menthol, herbs and liquorice overwhelmed her nose.

"My soothing ointment," Ig explained as he lathered a generous amount onto Smudge's wing. He then unwound a linen strap from his satchel and tied the wing to Smudge's body. "I've made some study of sprains and ailments. And no matter what Dr. Tundson says, there are ways to dress a sprain that are better than others. The key is to make sure there is compression, so it's not agitated and cool to reduce swelling. There."

He stood back, and they both admired his handiwork. Smudge gazed back at them with dark eyes, unphased by his new bandage.

"Thank you."

"Not a problem. What use is learning if you can't help people? Now then, where were we? Ah yes, locks…"

Crimson nodded politely as the discourse on locking mechanisms continued all the way through town. Although, Ig stuttered as they passed the blacksmith's and he nodded at the large minotaur beating a sheet of metal with a huge hammer, sending ringing beats out across the town. On closer inspection, Crimson realised that the hammer was attached to a metal fixing that replaced one of his hands.

"Who's that?" she asked.

"Milus." There was an edge of a wistful sigh in Ig's voice.

"You like him."

"What?" Ig's feathers bristled and he twisted his head around. "Who told you?" he hissed.

"You did. Why don't you go and talk to him?"

Ig shook his head. "We're at a very specific stage in our relationship. Besides I have a plan."

"And that is?"

"I continue to nod at him, and he nods at me and then, one day, after about another year, we progress to saying hello."

"That is a slow courtship."

"Keep your voice down!" The owl-like creature's feathers were now fluffed out so much he looked like a walking ball. "It's not a courtship. A courtship requires two people to like each other. Milus doesn't even know I exist. Except he must do, since we nod at each other. But he's not interested in me."

"How do you know?"

"Evidence. If he was interested, he'd say something."

"But you're interested in him, and you haven't said anything."

Ig gave a soft hoot. "Perhaps there is something to your theory. But I can't study it now, there's too much to do."

"Like making tea?"

"Tea is vital. But I was thinking of these dyes you're so keen to see."

Crimson bit her lip. Don't anger the helpful tylluan. The owl had claws, after all.

After a brisk walk, they ended up at the edge of a large river that flowed downhill and around the forest. Crimson shuddered, hoping no unicorns would venture out to meet them.

"Behold! The Rainbow River."

Crimson frowned. As with much of Saffron Vale, she was disappointed. There was no colour to the water. It was a normal river. Perhaps the water was clearer than she was used to in Oasis – she could see the bottom of the river here and a few fish darted around.

Two men sat on the riverbank, fishing poles in hand.

"Caught anything?" she asked as they passed.

"Nowt today, but a few salmon." One of them held up a brace of fish, gleaming in the midday sun.

"Old Man Rainbow's still eluding us. You don't fancy conjuring up one of your inny-ventyuns to help us get him, do you, Iggy?"

"I wouldn't risk getting on his bad side."

"Who's Old Man Rainbow?" Crimson asked.

"The largest rainbow trout to swim in this fair river. Rumour has it that he's the river guardian if you believe that sort of thing. Those two have been trying to catch him for years, but if he does exist, he's a wily creature and eludes capture. Now, this way."

Ig took them uphill to where different sized pools had been dug out near the river and a complicated system of gates either allowed water in or out or stopped it. Each of the pools sported a different colour, and below the surface, cloths bobbed.

This was where the magic of dyeing happened. But Crimson still had a question. "Why is it called Rainbow River?"

Ig blinked. "Isn't it obvious?"

Crimson shook her head.

"It's to do with the dyes. Now, look, this is my pool." He pointed to a small pool lined with white clay where bright yellow water lapped against the sides. "I've weighted the cloth for full absorption, and this is the third dye for extra staying power."

"How do you get it so bright?"

"A combination of bog myrtle, weld, and chalk. And of course, the quality of the cloth has a bearing on the depth of colour. I weave my own."

"Is there anything you can't do?"

Ig thought for a long moment, then shook his head. "I need to think about it properly. I expect there are many things, making instant tea for one, but to be able to answer accurately, I'd need to list out every possible thing that can be done and—"

"It was an expression."

"Oh, right." Ig took a book and piece of charcoal out of his satchel and wrote something down.

"What's that?"

"My social book. I write down expressions I haven't heard of and social niceties. I'm determined to crack the problem of etiquette and handling social situations. There must be a formula."

Crimson smiled. She'd never met anybody who thought like Ig. "So, can I buy the cloth from you?"

"Oh, no."

"Buy why?" Crimson felt all her hopes sinking away again.

"Because it's not ready. It needs a much longer soak and I was thinking of adding a fourth dip."

"Right, but when it's done, can I buy it? And I'll take any other cloth you have ready."

"Of course."

Crimson breathed out a sigh of relief. But there was still something bothering her, something that needed to be addressed. "How much is it?"

Ig blinked as if money wasn't something he ever considered. "Just have it. What use is it to me once I've proven the dye recipe?"

"Ig, I have to pay you." It went against all Crimson's learning at her old mentor's house to take something for free. Everything was paid for, and if it wasn't with money, it was with barter and if it was none of those things, then she should be very cautious. She didn't think the owl-like man was a teg trying to trick her into eternal bondage, but one couldn't be too careful[3].

"If you insist, usually I leave all that to Hardy. Take it up with him."

---

[3] And she was right to be cautious. The tale of Finnheart the Unwise tells of a young human who gives his name to a teg in exchange for gold and is then condemned to wander nameless, unrecognised by his friends and family and unable to get lodgings, until he begs the teg to take him to another realm. The story is wrapped up with a neat moral about the danger of strangers, but as with most tales, it has a grain of truth at its core. And is one of many stories where people are told not to trust tegs.

Chapter 13

~ *Luck spider* ~

HAVING SOLVED THE PROBLEM of having no cloth, and negotiating a fair price with Hardy on Ig's behalf, Crimson resolved to tackle her main problem; the shop.

True to her word, Dilly had brought round a bucketful of cleaning supplies, and Crimson tied a hideous apron around her waist. She didn't expect an apron to be glamourous, but this was drab and had strange frills attached to the edging and at random intervals over the fabric.

And there were no pockets. Most impractical. Maybe she should add a line of apron-wear to her clothing options. Crimson's head filled with possibilities. There was no reason why workwear had to be boring, as long as the fabric was practical and hardwearing. And darker colours might hide stains for longer than the plain linen. Each one could have a contrasting pocket for keeping dusters and other useful items close to hand.

She grabbed her design book and sketched out the shape with lists of ideas in a frenzy, taking a double page spread as she considered how straps could be attached with D rings. It was only when she looked up that she realised the best designs in the world couldn't be completed in a dirty, leaking room.

With a final scribble, she packed her book back in the satchel and grabbed a duster.

"So, it's really happening?"

Crimson whirled at the voice from her window and glared at Lief. "Don't you have work to do?"

He nodded. "But I couldn't miss seeing you cleaning. This ought to be good."

With a snort of irritation, Crimson stood on her tiptoes and angled the feather duster to reach as high into the room as she could. She missed the ceiling by about a foot. Annoyed, but not willing to ask for more help from the man who seemed determined to see her fail, she carried on. She could borrow a ladder later.

As she reached a corner, a small silver spider, no bigger than her thumb, descended from the ceiling. Crimson shrieked in surprise at its sudden appearance and went to swipe it away with the duster, intending to put it outside with all the other creepy crawlies.

"Stop!" There was genuine panic in Lief's voice.

Crimson raised an eyebrow and turned to him. "It's alright,

I'll just put it outside. You're not scared of spiders, are you?"

"No. No!"

"He who protests too much…"

"I am not protesting." Lief was inside now, and the room felt uncomfortable and small with his presence next to her. Crimson shifted from foot to foot. "It's a luck spider."

He picked it up with reverence and held it to the light. Its silver back shone and there was a small marking, like a four-leaf clover on its rounded back. It turned in a circle on his hand but made no move to escape.

"I've never seen one this close up before." He marvelled at the small creature.

"Spiders are only lucky for eating flies, and flies are not my problem here. The cobwebs are." Crimson frowned at the small-town superstition. Next, he'd say that she had to move out and leave the entire house to the spiders.

"Luck spiders choose where they live and give good fortune to any house they make their home. And it's going to take you a lot of good fortune to turn this place around."

Crimson held out her hand next to Lief's, ignoring the flare of heat that flamed where their skin touched. Probably an aftereffect of cleaning. The spider scurried onto her palm, tickling her skin with its short legs until it made it to the centre, where it sat looking up at her with large black eyes as round as beads.

Smudge roused himself from the corner and gave the small spider a sniff and a gentle lick with his long tongue before retreating to his bed. That settled it.

"Alright, he can stay." Lief was right. She needed all the luck she can get. "But only in one corner. Is that alright, Mr Spider?" The spider said nothing.

"And you must be tired of all these extra cobwebs. How about if I get rid of them and you can make a new home? A fresh start."

Again, the spider remained silent. Did they even speak? But it made no move to leave so Crimson handed the duster to Lief. He stared at it.

"Well, go on. You're the one who wanted me to make it a nice place for spiders. I can't reach the corners."

"You want me to dust for you?"

"The sooner you clear a space for Lucky, the sooner I can pop him back and get on."

He huffed out a snort of annoyance, but dusted all four corners in record time.

Crimson held her hand as high as it would go, and they both watched the spider climb onto the wall and up into the newly dusted corner. In no time at all, it had strung a compact web of thin, bright spider silk. A sunbeam caught the thread and refracted into a glistening rainbow of colours along the silk.

She gasped. This was a good omen for her work and, if the superstitions were true, the start of some good fortune.

"There, now he has a space." Crimson smiled.

The spider worked across the web and a word appeared in the silk, shining like silver; 'she'. Crimson frowned at the word. Did luck spiders communicate by writing in webs? That wasn't possible, was it? She squinted at the web. Must be a coincidence.

"Well, what do you know? She feels at home." Crimson decided not to comment on the writing, in case Lief thought she was mad. Instead, she wiped her hands on her apron and retrieved the duster from Lief who stood gawping at the web.

"He wrote a word." So, he could see it too.

"She wrote a word. Apparently. Maybe it's a trick of the light." But Crimson was sure it was genuine. Maybe the spider could pass on lucky messages through the web.

"I thought it was just stories." Lief still gazed up at the corner, his features so full of childlike wonder that Crimson couldn't help but stare. The hardy woodsman who hated outsiders was gone and, in his place, stood someone as amazed by simple things as she was, someone who saw the wonder in a bleak world. And that was someone she thought she could like. Or at least get on with. Where had 'like' come from?

"Well, she does. If she says anything about you, I'll let you know." Crimson's tone was brusque, annoyed at her treacherous mind for harbouring thoughts that weren't her own. Maybe the dust was getting to her. Yes, that was it. Too many new experiences and too much dust.

Lief turned away from the web with some reluctance, his features closing down so fast that Crimson wondered if she'd imagined the curiosity written there before.

"Maybe you will make it here, Red. If you've got luck on your side."

Before she had a chance to answer, he strode out and back up the ladder. Somehow, the hammering sounded louder through the empty shop than before.

Chapter 14

~ *A mix up of pies* ~

FTER A HARD DAY'S cleaning, Crimson stretched her shoulders. The front room looked a lot better. Of course, there was still loads to do. The wood needed sanding and coating, the cupboards needed refitting, the hole in the roof was smaller but still there, the shutters needed rehanging, the window needed fresh glass. And that was this room.

She hadn't dared go back to the kitchen or risk the death stairs to explore the room above the shop. Crimson yawned. It was exhausting remodelling a shop.

Smudge wandered over from the spot he had claimed as his own and nosed her hand before heading for the discarded sandwich wrapper from this morning.

"Sorry, boy, we haven't had a chance to eat all day. Why

don't we make up for it now?"

Dilly had promised her something at the end of the day, and she was too tired to refuse an offer of help. Crimson trudged her way to the bakery, marvelling at how the street that had streamed with water in the storm now sparkled in the weak afternoon sun. Even the fishy smell had lessened, no longer threatening to choke her every time she inhaled. Smudge bounded at her feet, chasing dragonflies and other insects.

The town bustled with locals going about their business, shouting greetings, and sharing gossip. It was a smaller version of home. A pang tugged at Crimson's chest. Oasis wasn't her home anymore, and she had to remember that. It was simply the place where she'd grown up. Getting away from the city and its limitations was the reason she had left. Here, she could be whoever she wanted, do whatever she wanted.

Her stomach growled. And what she wanted now was some food. She headed for the Cozy Lobster Bakery, next door to the Cozy Lobster café. It had the same red sea creature logo painted outside and Crimson inhaled the fading scent of baking bread and stepped inside.

A male version of Dilly smiled from behind the counter. They had to be related. Even the twist of their horns were the same.

"What can I get you for?" he asked, putting down his copy of The Golden Acorn newspaper and resting his huge hands on the polished countertop as he beamed at her.

"Dilly said to come by at the end of the day."

The horned man frowned, and Crimson's heart sank. Dilly had made a throwaway comment, and, like a fool, Crimson had taken her at her word.

She opened her mouth to ask for a loaf of bread and something for Smudge when the man smacked himself on the head.

"You must be the new member of the Shopkeepers Association."

"Er…"

"New to town, aren't you?"

"Yes."

"I knew it." He tapped the side of his nose. "I can always tell. Is that a dragon?"

"This is Smudge. He's staying with me for a while."

"Never heard of a pet dragon before. Does he bite?"

"No." Crimson crossed her fingers as the petalborn reached down to tickle Smudge under his chin. The small dragon wriggled with pleasure and licked his hand.

"I'm Duncan. Dilly said we were to help you out while you found your feet. Let me see what we've got here." He opened the door to a large oven built into the back wall of the shop and poked inside with an enormous wooden paddle. "My last two pies. Here, you have this one. It's chicken. The other is on order."

"Thank you. How much do I owe you?"

"On the house. Look, I burned the crust so can't sell it."

Duncan winked.

One edge of the pie was a little darker than the rest, but it wasn't burned. Crimson smiled back. "That's so kind."

Crimson took the pie and headed back to the shop, her mouth watering at the thought of moist chicken and buttery pastry. She stopped off at the town's shared water pump to fill up a jug for the night, saying hello to the townsfolk who didn't have plumbed in water supplies.

As she waited in line, she heard snippets of conversation.

"…Maire's latest obsession."

"It'll be the double decker carts all over again."

"He thinks he can change the transport system across the queendom."

"He can't even change the bed sheets."

The group in front of her finished up allowing Crimson to get her water to take home, where she used the paper wrapping as a plate – the kitchenware was still out of bounds until she could wash it – and cut into the pie.

She fed a piece to Smudge, who gobbled it up and then helped herself. It was delicious, still warm and homey. But it wasn't chicken.

Crimson studied the pastry lid and saw the number '7' stamped into the crust. She had someone else's pie.

It was an honest mistake on Duncan's behalf, but there was someone out there who had expected this pie and instead had her chicken one. She decided to at least tell Duncan.

"Looks like we're going out again, Smudge."

The energetic dragon jumped at her feet.

"I'm sorry, you can't have any more until I've told Duncan."

She raced back to the bakery and found Dilly and Duncan nursing mugs of tea. Both petalborns leaned forward and Crimson blinked away the thought that she was seeing double.

"Is something wrong with the pie?" asked Dilly.

"No, it's delicious," Crimson panted as she caught her breath. "But I don't think it's my pie."

"What do you mean?" asked Duncan.

"It's not chicken."

Duncan's brow furrowed in confusion.

"And there's a '7' on the lid."

Duncan smacked himself on the forehead, and Dilly swatted his arm. "It's not a seven, it's an 'L'. This was on order."

"My twin brother must have given you the wrong pie." Dilly rolled her eyes.

"It's OK, I can walk an apology basket up. We'll have to miss another games night, but–"

"I'll do it," Crimson volunteered.

The siblings stared at her.

"We couldn't," said Duncan at the same time as Dilly said, "Would you?"

"Of course. You should enjoy your games night. I don't have anything to do this evening and I owe you for the pie. Please, let me help."

"If you're sure…"

"I am."

"Right then." Dilly rubbed her hands together and called out items for the basket.

Crimson's head swam as they added jars of chutney and medlar jelly alongside scones, bread and salted butter. It seemed a lot to make up for a wrong order, but the twins were generous – they'd let her have a free pie after all. In a matter of moments, Duncan pressed a stuffed wicker basket into Crimson's arms and balanced the partly eaten pie on top before covering it with a tea towel the same bright red as the Cozy Lobster's painted sign.

"Thank you so much. We haven't had a games night in three months. You should come to the next one."

Duncan nodded in agreement.

Crimson took a step out of the door before she realised she had no idea where she was going. "Who's the delivery for?"

"Our local warden, Lief."

Chapter 15

~ The delivery ~

CRIMSON MUTTERED UNDER HER breath as she stomped out towards the woods to Lief's house. Typical. The order would belong to him. She'd only just escaped his superior smugness and sarcastic comments, and now she had to go to his house and apologise on behalf of the twins. They'd been kind enough to give her directions and offer to take it, but she'd felt bad for causing trouble and besides, she'd made the offer and she kept her word.

She was so caught up in her annoyance that she didn't register the house until she was at the doorstep.

He lived in a wooden house, built of sturdy weathered logs. A set of carved steps led up to a cheery green front door, a shade lighter than the pine trees in the forest that sprawled behind it. The roof was covered in mosses of every colour and the house was set into a small hillock, blending with the wild landscape.

Wind whipped round her, threatening to send the basket tumbling to the ground. This was a wild place, and she would do well to get out of there as soon as she could, but…there was something almost inviting about it. As if whoever had built it knew how to live with nature and was comfortable with its untamed wildness.

Smudge whined, and she shook herself. Best to get this over with. Balancing the basket on her hip, she rapped on the door.

She rearranged the checked tea towel with her free hand as she waited. A scraping sound inside told her someone was on the way and then Lief's familiar face appeared in the window. She heard his loud sigh before he shot the bolt and opened the door, filling the entrance with his large frame.

"I'm not working on your house tonight, Red. I have a life, you know."

"I can see. It must be difficult to pull yourself away from an evening grouching on your own."

His lips twitched. "How do you know I'm on my own?"

"Please."

The smell of apples hung around him, mixing with the woody scent of the forest, the salt of the sea and something baking.

"What do you want, Red?"

Crimson thrust the basket at him. "I came to give you this. On behalf of the Cozy Lobster."

His eyebrows raised.

"There was a mix up with the pies. I got yours – it's delicious by the way – but they wanted to apologise only they couldn't come themselves, so I said I would. I have the rest of the pie if you want it…" She trailed off, aware that she was babbling. "Could you take the basket so I can go?"

He leaned forward and lifted the cloth, examining the contents without taking it from her. Crimson pursed her lips. Of course, he would make her wait out here in the wind while he stood basking in the warmth of his cabin.

She shivered as he studied the jar of medlar jelly, then folded back the paper that surrounded the pie.

"You started eating it."

"I didn't realise it was yours until I took a bite and noticed it wasn't chicken."

"Why didn't you finish it?"

"I can't take something that belongs to someone else."

"There's far too much food here." He stepped back.

Crimson's jaw dropped. "You're not going to take it?"

"Far too much food for one person." He turned and walked back into the house.

Crimson stood there. What should she do? Leave the basket on the doorstep and go? Take it with her and explain to the twins?

"Bring it in, then."

Smudge darted in, making her decision for her. Crimson

didn't care for his tone, but the sooner she dropped off the apology basket, the sooner she could leave.

She stepped inside and headed for the large table, where she placed the basket and stood back to admire it. It really was a lot of food. Her stomach rumbled. The door shut behind her with a click.

Chapter 16

~ *A dinner invitation* ~

CRIMSON SPUN ROUND AND swallowed hard.

Lief had an odd look on his face.

She was trapped. In here. With a man she didn't even know. What was she thinking? This was exactly how people went missing in the murder mystery books her former employer's wife enjoyed. And she was an outsider. No one would care. No one from Oasis would even realise until months later, they would assume she was just too busy to write.

She pressed herself against the table, her knuckles turning white. If only she hadn't come in. If only she had inherited magic rather than her petite size from her teg heritage.

Smudge sat by the fire, turning hopeful eyes on her and Lief as he looked from the food to the people who could give it to him. Traitor.

Resolve sharpened, damping down the dragons that swarmed in her stomach, Crimson snatched up something heavy from the basket and held it out in front of her. She wouldn't go down without a fight.

"I think we should save the medlar jelly for after, don't you?" Lief went to a kitchen and retrieved three plates, setting them on the table next to the basket.

"W-what?"

"For after dinner." He gave her a look that said he thought she was slow or mad.

"Dinner?" Crimson's knees trembled as the adrenaline drained from her body. She wasn't going to die.

"You know, where you eat food. In the evening."

"You want me to stay for dinner?" With shaky hands, she placed the jar of jelly on the table.

Lief shrugged.

"But…why?" Crimson blurted out the words before thinking. She sounded rude and ungrateful. It might be a valid question – he'd made no secret that he thought she'd fail at her business – but she was hungry, and Smudge needed to eat. Even now, the dragon made small whimpering noises as he gazed up with his amber eyes, drool slipping from his mouth in long strands.

"I told you. There's too much food for one person. You're hungry, aren't you?"

With unerring timing, Crimson's stomach growled again.

A smug smile spread over Lief's face. "That's what I thought. Sit. Wipe the drool from your chin. I'm not going to kill you."

Crimson let out a forced laugh. His words were too close to her thoughts, and she shifted uncomfortably on her feet before sitting down.

Lief cut them both generous slices of each pie and poured two glasses of cloudy liquid that smelled of apples mixed with the yeasty must of beer.

"What does he eat?" He pointed a thumb at Smudge.

"He seems to eat anything."

Lief grunted and cut some more pie for the third wooden plate and placing it on the floor. Smudge tucked in with noisy gusto.

Crimson took a sip of the cider. It slipped down her throat with ease, tasting of apples but sharper. After the third sip, her body relaxed.

"Eat," said Lief through a mouthful of crumbs.

Crimson did. The pie was still scrumptious, and she felt her worries melt away as she took in the décor now she wasn't worried about getting murdered.

The walls were unlined wooden logs, but polished to a honey sheen that gave the house a sense of comfort in contrast with the rugged exterior. A fire burned in the stove, heating the open plan living room and kitchen to a comfortable warmth. A tasteful canvas of a field of purple flowers hung on the wall.

"That's gorgeous." Crimson stood to get a better look at the detail. "Who painted it?"

"A local artist." Lief eyed her as she studied the painting. It must mean a great deal to him if he was that nervous that she might touch it.

Crimson moved away from the artwork. A patched leather armchair sat near the fire with leatherwork hung over one arm.

"You sew?" Crimson asked, trying to reconcile her livelihood with the rough man who looked down on her.

"Only leather. When I need to. Who else would patch my boots?"

The cobbler. Crimson didn't voice the thought. He must be poor indeed to mend his own shoes. "Sensible." She changed the subject. "This is a lovely home."

Lief grunted.

"So clever to stay with wooden hues all around, so many different browns." Crimson took them all in. The pine of the table they sat at, just a shade lighter than the tea brown of the knots in the walls, which themselves were a shade darker than the honey walls. And matching floors, scuffed with daily use. It was warm and cozy and filled with a homeliness that made her want to stay.

"Thank you."

There was something in Lief's tone that made Crimson cock her head. "Did you build this?"

Lief nodded, shovelling more food into his mouth.

"It's…impressive."

"I'm good with my hands."

What could she say to that? "So am I."

Lief studied her for a long moment and Crimson felt her face heat. So she fought back before he could say something to catch her off-guard. "You have crumbs in your beard."

He wiped them away with a cocky smile. "Were you looking at my mouth?"

"No. I just couldn't miss the second meal you had stuck around it."

Lief laughed at that. Crimson smiled too. This man brought out a snipy side to her that she didn't know existed, but it was fun needling him, knowing he could take a joke.

Smudge nosed at her knee, and she fed him some more food.

"You know, a coastal dragon's place is in the wild, not scavenging for scraps under a table. He'd be happier where he's meant to be, back in his natural habitat."

Crimson shrugged. "He doesn't seem to mind."

Smudge snorted in agreement and begged for more food.

Lief's lips scrunched together in judgement.

"I can't abandon him to the wild; his wing is injured. He'll never make it."

Lief sighed and relented. "I suppose. But when he's healed, you should take him to the dragon colony out on Wyrm Rock so he can be with others of his own kind. It's not natural for him to be on his own. May I?" He gestured to Smudge's bandage and Crimson nodded.

She leaned back as she watched him unravel it, study the injury then reset it with a practised hand while he crooned a soothing song to the small dragon.

"I'll think about taking him to that rock," Crimson promised. "But for now…" She fed him another morsel and Smudge sat next to her looking smug and content. She scratched his head. He didn't seem like a wild dragon, but Lief was more used to fierce creatures.

"Do you have much experience with dragons?"

"They're part of my remit." That didn't clear anything up.

"What is it that you do?"

"I'm a warden. I look after the vale, protect it from any threats to our way of life." His gaze rested on her for a long beat.

Crimson coughed to ease some of the tension that bubbled under her skin at his gaze. "Then it's a good job there are no threats here."

He nodded. She reached for a scone, slathering it with jam and butter. Crimson groaned in pleasure as she the heady combination of cake, medlar jelly, and salted butter melted in her mouth.

"Well now I have to try that too," Lief said, preparing his own scone. "Darn, that's good. Only thing better is scones with clotted cream."

"So good. I might have to ask Duncan for the recipe." Not that she had the first idea how to cook.

"I might have to ask Duncan to marry me, then he can cook

scones for me."

Crimson gave the kitchen an assessing look. "No, he'd never agree to marry someone with such a small kitchen."

"You've been here less than two days, and you know what he'd like?"

She'd meant it as a joke. Crimson bristled. "I know more about people than you."

"Really?"

"Yes, really. Even the moons choose to share the sky with each other. You choose to live apart, away from everyone."

Lief stiffened in his chair before standing up. "Time to go, Red."

"Oh, yes, right. Thank you for the food," Crimson said, unsure what had happened. One minute they were talking like normal people, like friends even, and now he wanted to throw her out. Into the dark. Alone.

Lief sighed. "Come on, I'll walk you back."

He lit a lantern and opened the door, gesturing for her to go. Crimson considered turning him down, but the unicorn loomed large in her mind and she stayed silent.

Crimson called Smudge, and they set off into the dark night. At the first curve in the path, Crimson looked back at Lief's home.

The plain, wooden shutters were pulled tight against the darkening evening, keeping in the warmth. As she looked back at the chinks of light from the banked fire peeping through the small gaps around the window and door, she acknowledged that it had been an enjoyable evening. Until he'd thrown her out. Or rather, until she'd said something that had messed up the evening. Would she ever fit in here?

Now she wasn't frightened for her life, the cottage looked like something out of a storybook. She snuck a glance at the tall figure walking at her side. And Lief was less of a big bad wolf and more of the rugged woodsman who came to the rescue.

Warm contentment spread through her, maybe they could get along and even be friends. After all, he was walking her home.

They stopped outside her door, and Crimson fumbled in her pocket for the key.

Lief started walking back.

"Wait."

He turned. The lantern threw up menacing shadows on his face, but his impatient eyebrows were clear.

"I can't see." The excuse sounded lame even to her ears. She wanted him to stay. Just for a moment more. Why? She had no idea. Earlier this evening she thought he wanted to kill her, but maybe something had shifted in the time they spent together.

With an ineloquent grunt, he thrust the lantern at her and headed into the night.

"But how will you find your way?" Crimson called after him.

"I have excellent night vision," he said without turning back.

That put her in her place. With a sigh, Crimson went inside and locked up.

"At least you like me," she said, stroking the small dragon's head before curling up on her makeshift bed. Well, now she knew for sure. Lief didn't like her, didn't want to be friends, and wanted her to fail. She couldn't ignore him; they had to work together on the shop. So she would be civil, but she couldn't let her guard down. She had to focus on her business and showing people her creativity.

Chapter 17

~ *The kitchen* ~

A WEEK LATER AND the shop had undergone a radical transformation. The roof was patched, the shutters rehung and though the glass in the window hadn't yet been replaced, it had been ordered. On the inside, the luck spider now presided over a clean space and Crimson had refitted the cupboards and hung shelves under Lief's instructions.

The freshly waxed wood gave a golden glow to the interior, the perfect setting for her creations. When she had the time and space to create anything.

Ig's fabric sat in neat bolts on the new shelves, waiting to be transformed into clothes. Crimson's head spun with ideas and her design book filled fast with sketches. She had persuaded Ig to make her some inks in the same colour as the material and the colours were so bright, her heart sung when she used them, testing different combinations for maximum impact.

She stared at them now while she waited for Lief. Late. Again. The man worked to his own time with no regard for anyone else. It was no wonder that he was alone.

A cough drew her from her book.

"If you're ready to get started, Red?"

"I was waiting for you."

"I thought it was rude to interrupt someone while they were reading. What are you reading anyhow? Some sappy romance?"

"What? No!" Not that she didn't enjoy a sappy romance novel – they were her favourite type of book, actually – but this was work. "And it's none of your business."

Crimson realised her mistake as soon as she said the words. She'd piqued his interest. He stepped up to her shoulder just as she slammed the book shut and placed it on the table.

"Shall we start?"

"Of course." He snatched the book up and opened it. "As soon as I see what's so interesting."

Crimson fought the urge to reach for her design book. She wasn't ashamed of her sketches, and one of them had to act like an adult.

"You really are a seamstress, then?"

"Of course," her brow crinkled, "I said I was a dressmaker. What else would I be?"

He didn't answer, but just gave her a look that told her she was stupid. Crimson blushed. He couldn't mean what she thought he meant, could he? Well, she wasn't going to rise to the bait and ask him.

"If you've finished with my book. We've got a lot of work to do."

"You're the boss."

"I am." She squared her stance, channelling whatever scrap of confidence she had left. "And today we're tackling the kitchen. And I want to look upstairs."

"What's stopping you?"

"Woodworm."

He nodded and strolled into the kitchen. Crimson waited for the flap of pigeon wings and a satisfied smile crept over her lips at his curse of surprise.

"Watch out for the pigeon," she said in a sing-song voice before joining Lief in the kitchen.

"That's the first thing to go. Animals belong in the wild."

"Go on, then."

He arched a brow at her.

"You live in the forest; you're used to dangerous animals."

"A pigeon isn't what I'd call dangerous."

"You haven't seen them mug a tourist who didn't eat their sandwich fast enough." Crimson shivered at the memory.

There had been so many of them, ducking and diving at the poor fellow and his daughter. Screams. Specks of blood. The evil birds only stopped when the man had the presence of mind to throw the bread so they could escape.

Oblivious to her distress, Lief tried the back door. It didn't budge. He leant his shoulder against the wood and heaved until it opened with a splintering crack.

Crimson pursed her lips. Another problem. This entire shop was problem after problem, and she couldn't start making any stock until it was all sorted. She was caught in a web of problems. As soon as one got fixed, another took its place. Crimson began listing them in her mind; twenty-two. Caught in twenty-two problems.

Lief waved his arms, his huge form filling the space as he chased the pigeon out with a series of shouts and gestures. The pigeon eyed him with dumb, red eyes before cocking its head like this was all too much trouble and flying out.

One problem solved.

Her gaze lit on the lock. Still twenty-one to go.

"I'll fix the lock," Lief said.

Crimson forced herself to look at the positives. The pigeon was gone at least. She clapped her hands together. "Excellent start. Now, if you can fix the tap, I can start washing while you rehang the doors."

"Shouldn't be a problem. What have we got here?" Lief stepped up to the tap and pumped the handle.

A strange grumbling sound rang through the pipe.

"Sounds like a blockage somewhere…" He bent down and put his head under the faucet. And was rewarded with a spurt of sludge all over his face.

Crimson laughed. She couldn't help it. His serious,

handsome face was coated with disgusting slime that even now filled the room with an awful smell somewhere between a blocked drain and stale cabbage.

"Are you laughing at me?"

Crimson's shoulders wobbled. "No." She dissolved back into giggles. It wasn't even that funny, but she couldn't stop. It was like a tap had turned on inside her body and it shook with release as she bent over and fought to get her breath back through the laughter.

Lief's lips curved into a wicked smile.

As Crimson wiped tears from her eyes, he flung a handful of the slimy sludge at her. "My hair!" She stopped laughing in an instant, putting her hands up to her filthy locks.

"I can see what was so funny," Lief snorted.

Crimson grabbed as much of the slime as she could out of her sensible ponytail and stepped towards him, aiming to transfer it back onto him.

He grabbed her hands with a simple movement and held her while she pulled against him. "Let me go!" she panted.

"Are you going to slime me?"

She paused. "Maybe."

"Then I'm not letting you go."

The smug tone of his voice fuelled the spark of rebellion in her. While he focused on her hands, she leaned in and smeared what was left of the mess in her hair onto his shirt.

"Very clever." He released her hands.

She blinked up. Had she gone too far? And she'd ruined his shirt. What if he didn't have another? He lived in that ramshackle place in the forest, not in town. Oh stitches, what had she done?

But he was smiling. She smiled back. And he pumped the tap again, sending a shower of mucky water into the sink onto his hand, which he angled so it sprayed her.

"Argh!"

She threw her hands up and turned so she was side on – a smaller target for the soaking.

"Are we done?"

"Yarg," she gargled through the water.

Lief nodded.

Crimson squinted at him, wiping water from her face. She wanted to stay angry, but it was all just too funny. They dissolved into laughter and once again Crimson thought they could be friends.

"That's the tap sorted." Crimson considered changing but her only other dress wasn't suited to housework so her only options were to carry on in her wet attire or strip down to her linens.

Probably not a good idea considering how see through linen got when it was wet. Her gaze flicked to Lief, who leaned against a counter, dripping onto the floor. His shirt clung to his skin and Crimson looked away, heat flooding her face.

Best to stay in her sodden dress.

She rolled up her wet sleeves and got to work.

A few hours later and the kitchen was unrecognisable. It sparkled.

Crimson stretched, working a kink from her back and shoulders. Cleaning was hard work.

Lief grunted as he fitted the last cupboard and wiped his brow with the back of his hand. Even though they had worked in near silence, it amazed Crimson that they hadn't got in each other's way. She had bustled around cleaning while he cleared the chimney, swept up the mess and rehung the wonky cupboard doors.

They had even set a small fire in the stove to boil water for tea in the newly cleaned kettle she had found in amongst the pots and pans. She set it to boil now and yawned, ready to collapse after the hard day's work. At her feet, Smudge curled close to the fire, soaking up all its warmth with contented snores.

Crimson opened a cupboard and gave a yelp of surprise. The demon pig duck stared back at her.

"By the moon, what is that atrocity?"

Crimson bristled at his dislike of the ceramic object. "It's not so bad…"

"It really is. You didn't pay money for that, did you?"

"I found it here."

"Makes sense. The previous owner might have moved out just to get away from it."

Crimson snorted a laugh and poured the tea into the two least cracked mugs she could find. "Who did live here? Before…?"

She gestured to the place.

"Not sure. It's been abandoned for years." Lief scratched his stubble. "Maybe a lady? I seem to remember she sold sweets when I was a kid. Dad used to slip me a silver to get some for me and my sister." He smiled into the distance.

That fit with what Dilly had said about the shop's previous owner. They sipped tea and debated the merits of butter mints compared to toffee chews as the afternoon drew on.

"There's still some daylight. Did you want to see upstairs?" he asked.

She nodded through the queendom's biggest yawn and moved over to the stairs. He started climbing without a care until his foot went through the fourth step.

"That'll be the woodworm," she said with an air of knowing.

"You think?" he snapped, and Crimson flinched. They had got on so well today that his flash of anger was a slap in her face. She had to remember that he was her employee. Not a friend. He made that clear. He snorted and yanked his leg free before stomping off.

Crimson sighed. She wasn't going to see upstairs today.

But Lief returned with his ladder and set it against the stairwell. "Go on then. I'll hold it."

She blinked away her surprise and heaved herself up the ladder, her shoulders protesting any movement.

Crimson peeped through the top rungs of the ladder. Her first impression was of space and dust. A few lazy rays of afternoon sun peeked through chinks in the wooden shutters from two windows. A double aspect. Perfect for a workshop.

She scrambled up and tested her weight on the boards. There was a small creak, but they held. Moving in the same tiptoe fashion, testing each part of the floor before she committed her full weight to it, she made it to a window and flung open the shutters.

The room flooded with light, making the dust suspended in the air glow like pixie dust. Exposed beams soared above her head in the large attic room, twice the size of her bedroom back at Senda's Emporium. Crimson smiled and tension left her shoulders. There was enough room for a single bed – no, a double. And she could work here in the evenings, cutting fabric and designing patterns after hours.

"Nice space."

Crimson jumped. For a large man, Lief moved with predatory silence. After swallowing the squeal of surprise that threatened to leap out of her throat, she said, "It's perfect. I can't wait to decorate."

"What colour are you thinking?"

Crimson tilted her head. She hadn't let herself picture colour on any of the walls. Senda's Emporium had white walls; the better to show off the merchandise. But this was her space. She could have anything she wanted…With a sigh, she said, "White. Better to catch the light so I can work longer."

"Life isn't all about work."

Crimson barked out a scoffing laugh. "What do you know about it?" She bit her tongue to stop herself from more cruelty.

"How would I even find paint? None of the buildings are painted. I thought it would be a riot of colour, but it's only the fabrics that are bright."

"You should see it later in the year, when the flowers come out. It's a sight to behold."

"I'll believe it when I see it."

"If you look down on the vale so much, why did you even come here?" With that, he marched back to the ladder and climbed down. "Come on, I've got things to do. Unless you want me to leave you up there."

Crimson closed the shutters with a click and hurried back downstairs. She had no doubt that he would follow through on his threat to abandon her upstairs.

"Good riddance," she muttered after he'd left.

She felt eyes on her and tilted her head so she could see the luck spider in its web. "Well, it is."

The spider scurried across the silver strands of its web and the words *good heart* appeared.

"Thank you. I try my best." That was the sort of encouragement she needed.

She headed back to the kitchen and smiled at all they'd done, breathing in the fresh scent of lavender and lemon from the cleaning fluid and missing the spider's second message of; *him.*

Chapter 18

~ *A short discussion on paint* ~

BUOYED BY THE CLEAN kitchen, Crimson decided to celebrate by going down to the pub.

On the corner of the high street, she spotted Ig gesticulating wildly with the maire, who far exceeded Ig's energy. Hardy skulked behind them, making notes and shaking his head.

"I'm telling you it won't work. The natural laws won't allow it–"

"Poppycock!" Maire Bowan interrupted Ig with a snort. "I'm talking about transforming our transportation system and you're throwing numbers at me."

"I've modelled it. It can't take the corners on streets this narrow."

"Then we'll widen the road."

Ig gave an exasperated hoot and gave Hardy a pleading look. The clerk shook his head and noted something down.

"I won't be part of this." Ig stalked off, his feathers raised. He almost collided with Crimson.

"Tough day?" she asked.

"Quite. He won't listen." The tylluan dragged his hand down his face.

"Want a drink?"

"Excellent idea. I know just the place."

Woolton had two pubs to choose from: the local branch of the Salt and Pickle chain renowned for good food and cosy rooms and an independent inn called the Drunken Gull.

As you already know, the latter squatted near the harbour, tiny windows keeping the weather out and the air of a place that didn't have to deal with 'artisanal menus' and 'craft beers'. In other words, it was a local pub, the sort of place where you could only be called a regular if your family had drunk there for three generations, and even then, some of the patrons might call you 'newbie'.

And it was here that Ig led them. Her first experience had been less than pleasant, but now she had been in Woolton for a while and met some welcoming people. She was almost a member of the Shopkeeper's Association, or she would be as soon as she opened her shop. It was time to prove she was a local.

As she walked along the street, she jerked to a halt at the sign pointing to Upper Gull's Bottom. So she hadn't misread it during the storm. Ig's head swivelled one hundred and eighty degrees to see why she'd stopped.

"Is that sign a joke?" she asked, not quite believing that anyone could name part of their town after a bird's posterior.

Ig pointed to another street sign opposite that indicated that there was a Lower Gull's Bottom, too. "Before Woolton expanded, there was a small hamlet here called Gull's Bottom. Why are your shoulders shaking? Is it funny?"

"I suppose not…" Shaking her head, she caught up with the tylluan.

As she neared the harbour, a pungent smell assaulted her nostrils. Fish and salt. A gull cawed from somewhere overhead, invisible in the storm. Would she ever get used to the stench that hung round the coastal town? So alien compared to what she'd known in the mountain city of Oasis. But at least the odour of raw sewage wasn't strong here. In the city, the drains often backed up from the multitudes of people living in close quarters. That was one benefit of being in a more rural vale.

Counting all the benefits of the vale, the largest one being that she no longer had to deal with her mentor, she pushed open the door and stepped into the Drunken Gull. There were fewer patrons sat round the wonky tables today, and this time, they gave the newcomers a cursory glance before turning back to their pints. Progress.

Ig strode to the bar and ordered something before heading to a small table in the corner.

The cyclops behind the bar eyed Crimson. "Is that a dragon?"

"Yes, he's well behaved."

"Make sure he doesn't burn anything."

"You have my word."

The bartender grunted in acknowledgement. "What you having?"

"Er, the same. Please."

The bartender grunted and pulled Crimson a half pint of brownish liquid with a foamy froth on top.

She sniffed it. "What's it called?"

A slow smile crossed the cyclops' face. "Dragon's Piss."

Charming. Crimson took her drink over to Ig's table, her cheeks heating in embarrassment at being the butt of a joke.

Moments later, the cyclops brought over two bowls of something that smelled like fish guts with a seaweed aftertaste that stung her nostrils. Can you get a seaweed aftertaste in the nose? Perhaps a seaweed aftersmell? Either way, it lingered.

The tylluan leant over his bowl and inhaled with a sigh of appreciation. "Excellent, as always Gruff."

"What's that?" Crimson asked once the bartender had left, breathing through her mouth.

"The special," replied Ig after he'd swallowed a spoonful that looked like it contained part of an octopus tentacle. "Best not to ask what's in it though." He sighed. "The chef won't reveal his recipe. I've been asking for years."

Crimson didn't know what to say to that, so she smiled. "Speaking of recipes, how's the dye coming along?"

"Oh yes, very well. It'll be ready soon and I've got the rest of the cloth as soon as you want to collect it."

Crimson sighed and drew a pattern on the wood with her finger, smearing a drop of leftover something across the surface before she thought better of it. Who knew what was in that liquid? And she daren't ask for a serviette in this place.

"I'll pick the fabric up soon. The shop's all clean, downstairs at least, but it could really do with a coat of paint before I start stocking anything."

Ig nodded around another mouthful of soup.

"I suppose I'll have to get some lime wash from somewhere. Unless you know of anywhere that sells paint?"

"For artwork?" He thought for a moment. "Sibby paints. They might have something. But they're out of town on a tour at the moment."

"I was thinking of an entire wall."

"That's a big canvas." Ig's hand stopped halfway between the bowl and his mouth; the spoonful of soup forgotten as a faraway look came into his huge eyes. "I suppose, with the right pigment and right solvents and binders, you could make a large quantity of paint. What colours were you thinking?"

"Er…"

"You're right! We shouldn't limit ourselves. I'll test them all."

"You want to make paint? For me?" Crimson wasn't sure

she'd heard him right.

"It's an avenue of pigmentation I haven't yet explored. We can start tomorrow. Join me at sunrise at the beach and we'll start with purple." Ig lifted his spoon to his mouth and slurped his soup.

"Do you want mine?" Crimson offered after taking a tiny sip of the soup. The fishy concoction tasted just as she imagined and it was either offer it to Ig or to Smudge and the latter felt impolite, even in a place like this.

Ig took her bowl and mumbled a thanks as he supped up a small fish head, complete with eyes and teeth.

She excused herself and went to the bar to ask for something else to eat when she felt eyes burning into her back. She turned to see Lief glaring at her.

She swallowed. Couldn't she escape him?

"Can't I get a drink in peace?" he asked, approaching the bar and taking a spot right next to her, leaning into her personal space.

"I didn't realise this was your private watering hole."

He narrowed his eyes.

Crimson ignored him and asked for some bread and cheese. The bartender grunted and handed her a cracked plate. She took it back to the table and angled her chair so her back was to the bar, determined not to let Lief cloud her evening.

But Lief didn't seem to have the same idea, because with a scrape of a chair, he sat himself at their table.

Crimson opened her mouth to protest but Ig welcomed him

like an old friend.

"How goes the wardening?"

"Good. Someone's got to protect this place from outsiders." He cut a look at Crimson.

Her cheeks flamed and she stuffed a piece of bread into her mouth, chewing with a ferocity she hadn't thought she possessed. This man brought out the worst in her and she wouldn't lose her friendship with Ig because she couldn't hold her tongue.

The tylluan frowned. "Protecting nature is the warden's code, is it not?"

Lief grunted and swirled his drink, spilling some of the frothy beer onto the table.

"And your…condition?"

Lief shifted in his seat. "Manageable."

So, he had some sort of illness. Crimson's heart panged with sympathy. That explained his surly behaviour; he was ill, perhaps in pain most of the time.

"Is there anything that can be done?" she asked.

"It's nothing to be ashamed of," Ig said.

"I don't want to talk about it," Lief said through gritted teeth. "Especially not with someone like you."

What did that mean? Crimson's sympathy disappeared in an instant. Maybe he had an embarrassing, uncomfortable condition like boils on his bottom. Her lips twitched as she imagined increasingly stupid diseases for him. Perhaps he had an extra set of toenails. On his bottom.

"Something funny, Red?"

Oh, stitches and pins. This wasn't her. Why did he grate on her so much? And now he had her thinking awful thoughts when he had a real illness that clearly caused him discomfort. She stood so hard that her chair fell backwards, clunking onto the tiled floor.

A cheer rang out around the bar as the patrons indulged in the tradition of pubs everywhere of making someone who's broken something or knocked something over the largest amount of embarrassment possible.

"I have to go." With that, she fled, stopping only to call Smudge after her.

Chapter 19

~ The Great Lobster ~

THE FOLLOWING MORNING, CRIMSON got up before sunrise. It wasn't a hardship. She'd hardly slept after her embarrassing display, coupled with shameful thoughts about Lief's bottom, which may or may not have been covered with oozing pustules.

She left her shop as the dove grey predawn broke into soft yellows and oranges. Smudge darted around at her heels, stopping to sniff interesting smells and add his own scent to the best spots.

Crimson rubbed her arms, wishing she'd brought her cloak. The wind would be lovely later when the sun was higher, but right now, in the coldness of after dark, it chilled her.

She kept her gaze away from the Drunken Gull as she hurried onwards to Ig's lighthouse, the stripy building imposing in the dawn light.

"Sorry," she said as soon as the tylluan had descended.

He tilted his head. "For what?"

"My behaviour last night."

"Is offering me your soup not acceptable friendship behaviour?" His brow creased, causing his feathers to crumple. "I shall have to write that down."

"Not for that. For being rude to Lief and then leaving without saying goodbye."

"I hadn't noticed. I thought the soup was particularly good yesterday. Did you notice how they'd browned the tentacles?"

"Er…"

"Anyway, we waste time while the tide is low. We must away." With that, he stuffed a satchel into her arms, flung one side of his brown cloak over his shoulder and set off in the direction of the beach.

Crimson hurried after him, tripping over her feet. "So, what are we looking for?"

"Myrrx shells."

"Bless you."

"No, myrrx shells."

"Shells?"

"For purple. I have almost every other pigment, except the saffron poppy." His large eyes misted over.

"Wait, you get royal purple from shells?"

"That is what I said." With that, Ig hopped over the wall and glided down to the beach, where he began sifting through debris with his fingers.

Crimson used the steps and caught up with him. "What do the shells look like?" she panted, hands on hips, catching her breath. Smudge raced off to chase the white gulls that picked over the seaweed.

Ig gave a hoot of triumph and held up a dark spiral shell with a gentle curve in it about the size of her hand. Crimson took it, feeling the ridged surface against her palm.

"But this is black."

"Look inside."

Crimson flipped the shell and gasped. The delicate inner lining shimmered in the morning light, catching pearlescent hues of lavender. She traced a finger over the concave shell, so smooth, it was almost like silk.

"How do you turn this into pigment?"

Ig dropped another shell into his bag. "I grind it up into a fine powder, which we can mix with the fixatives to create dye. But it takes a lot of shells to make a small amount of powder, about two hundred and fifty thousand for an ounce."

"That many?" They'd never find enough. And no wonder royal purple fabric was so expensive; she'd had no idea.

"I won't be able to make enough paint for the outside of your shop, but there should be plenty to add a little purple to the inside with what we find today. And if you find a living myrrx, let me know."

"I don't want to kill anything…"

"Who said anything about killing?" Ig hooted and bent down, picking through seaweed for more of the large shells.

Crimson placed the shell into her bag with reverence, still unable to believe that something so dark on the outside had such potential for brightness. But if it took so many shells to make such a small amount of purple, they needed to hurry.

Now that Crimson knew what the shells looked like, she found them with ease and ignored the slime of seaweed and the occasional dead fish washed up on the wrack line of the shore.

After an hour, her bag was stuffed, and she collapsed against a rock covered with barnacles.

"I think that's about all we can do for today," Ig said, "such a shame there were no living myrrx around, then we'd get much more colour."

"Living myrrx?" a deep voice boomed from the other side of the rock.

"Who's there?" Crimson scrambled up the rock, clutching her bag of valuable shells to her chest as she peered over the other side.

Under her feet, the mottled stone shifted. Two bulbous eyes on stalks unfolded themselves, one focusing on Ig and the other swivelling to stare at Crimson. "Would you mind getting off my shell? Only having my eye like this gives me a headache."

Crimson screamed, lost her balance, and landed on the sand with a thump.

The rock turned, revealing enormous claws and an ugly face filled with strange, spindly legs.

"Are you alright?" the rock said, clacking its mouthpieces together.

Crimson screamed again, scrambling backwards.

Ig bowed low. "Great Lobster. I didn't expect to see you here today."

"I didn't expect to find myself here either." The gigantic lobster made a croaking sound that may have been a laugh. "Must have got swept up with the tide."

"You know that…lobster?" Crimson whispered to Ig as he straightened and brushed some sand from his feathers.

"Hmm? Oh yes, we sometimes see each other when I'm out tracking tide movements or weather developments. The Great Lobster is something of an expert on weather patterns."

"I get a feeling in my left antenna, just above the bend."

"And I contest that it is not just a feeling, but something measurable."

"Aren't feelings measurable?" Crimson asked, bewildered by the conversation. And why not in both antennae? Would it be rude to ask? As Crimson debated, the conversation moved on.

"Exactly what I say," agreed the Great Lobster. "There is a great deal of difference between a squall and a full-blown storm. I feel it in my shell."

"But how?" Ig asked, and Crimson got the impression that she was caught in the middle of something that they had both discussed before. "If you would let me attach my new machine to your shell, maybe–"

"The last time you strapped something to my shell, it made me irresistible to the kraken."

"And now we know that the kraken responds to strong noises at that frequency. A fascinating discovery."

"Very well for you to say, but try fending off an amorous kraken. I had to swim all the way to Turtle Bay before I could scrape your contraption off."

"You told me it broke." Ig sounded both hurt and annoyed.

"It did. When I squashed it against a rock." The Great Lobster held up one of its enormous claws to stop Ig's protest. "Did I hear you say you were after myrrx?"

"Yes," Crimson said, taking over for Ig who kicked the sand with his feet and muttered something about weeks of research ruined.

"There's a rout of them in those rockpools, stranded by the high tide last night. Speaking of, I'd better get back under water before these gulls decide I'm fair game." With that, the gargantuan lobster heaved itself down the beach and disappeared into the sapphire sea, leaving a deep trail of whorls on the sand.

Crimson stared after the huge crustacean. "Was that real or am I dreaming?"

"Oh, they're real alright, a real pain. I spent weeks designing that speaker so it could play underwater and for what? Nothing."

"They said there were living myrrx over here."

"Hmm? Oh, right. Come on then, and grab that nori." Ig pointed to some seaweed on the sand.

"This?" Crimson grabbed a handful.

"No, the thin stuff, like paper."

Grabbing as much of the seaweed as she could, Crimson followed Ig to the rockpools. Small sand-coloured fish flitted between stones and bright anemones with flashes of their silver bellies. In the water and on the rocks were hundreds of snails, each with a dark shell and leaving trails of vibrant purple slime behind them.

As Crimson watched, they turned as one and headed for her with a low sucking, squelching noise. She backed away. Did every creature in this vale want to hurt her?

"Put the nori down." Ig took some from her and placed it on a smooth section of a slate grey rock. The sea snails changed direction and made their way to the closer pile of seaweed. Crimson breathed a sigh of relief. They wanted food, not her.

"Over there. That's it." Ig said, working with her to place all the seaweed on the stone. "Now we wait."

They didn't have to wait long. Soon enough, the rock glistened with purple slime as the myrrx – myrrxes? Myrrxi? Why were plurals so difficult? – devoured the seaweed with toothless mouths. Once the nori had completely disappeared, they slid back to the rock pool to await the return of the tide.

Ig produced a flask from somewhere under his cloak and handed it to Crimson. "If you would be so kind as to scrape the slime into here. I'd do it, but," he shrugged, "feathers."

Pulling a face, Crimson scooped up the gooey slime and scraped it into the flask. It was cold and mucus like and when she'd finished, her hands were coated with a thin layer of goo and stained a berry colour that she wasn't sure would come off.

"Excellent. That will help with both the richness of the colour and the amount I can make." Ig hooted happily. "Now, how about some tea?"

Crimson called Smudge over and he galloped over the sand in happy bounces to lay a dead fish at Crimson's feet.

"Er, well done?"

Smudge preened and gulped it down in two bites. He wagged his tail and Crimson patted his head before they headed back to Ig's for a cup of tea.

Chapter 20

~ *A surprise gift* ~

TEA WAS AN UNEVENTFUL affair. Ig didn't mention his tea-making invention, although Crimson noticed new shards of shrapnel and a fresh spout embedded in the plastered walls of his lighthouse.

He cleared a space for her to sit by sweeping a pile of certificates to the floor.

"Are you really a member of all these guilds?" Crimson asked as she caught glimpses of crests and calligraphed writing that signalled membership. A pang of envy rang through her head and settled in her chest. She hadn't even got into one guild thanks to a combination of her bold design choices and the betrayal of someone she'd considered her best friend, maybe even more than a friend…she shut that thought down before it could get any farther.

Ig waved a hand, dismissing his achievements. "I needed access to the archives to further my research. It seemed the easiest way. And you'd be amazed how eager they were to present me with membership, provided I corresponded with them from afar rather than attending in person."

Crimson raised an eyebrow, not sure what to make of that. Ig seemed alright to her, but for a guild to both want him as a member and tell him to never darken their sacred guildhalls…there must be something more to his studies and inventions.

But right now, her focus was on tea and breakfast as Ig placed two cups on a small circle of space amid the clutter, followed by a plate of buttered crumpets.

Crimson tasted the tea. Delicious. She caught sight of the crest of the Worshipful Tea Masters with its golden teapot pouring into a cup. That explained Ig's obsession with tea.

"Have you said anything to Milus?"

"What?" Ig fumbled with his cup. "Why would I have anything to say to our local blacksmith? Expert though he is with metallurgical works, I, myself, am capable of creating anything I need. Do you want to see my forge?"

"I meant maybe you should talk to him, see if he feels the same way about you."

"I told you, I have a system. It's all here." He pulled out a notebook and drew a clawed finger down a page. "The perfect formula for developing a relationship. Milus and I are at stage one; acknowledgement of existence. The next stage is acquaintance, followed by friendship at which stage I can determine if there is romantic interest by careful study of his physiological response to me without suffering embarrassment."

"Sounds exhausting."

"Nonsense. It's logical." Ig let out a soft hooting sigh. "Although I will admit that it would be far easier if there was an instant attraction. I have heard of the thunderbolt effect where two people are struck by the instant knowledge that they are made for each other. But, I fear I may overthink things, making me less susceptible to such a phenomenon. In fact, that would be an excellent study; a comparison of intelligence with speed of falling in love. Are you in love?"

Crimson choked on a mouthful of crumpet, sending a spray of buttery crumbs onto the floor where Smudge roused himself to lick them up. "What? No."

The last person she had feelings for had sold her out to get ahead and take a spot in the Dressmakers' Guild. She was here for her business, not for romance. Crimson frowned as she puzzled through the rest of his sentence. Was Ig suggesting she was stupid?

"Really? I observed a spark of strong emotion between you and Lief at the Gull last night."

"Strong emotion is not the same as love. If anything, what's between us is disinterested loathing."

"Loathing, you say?" Ig scribbled something down in his book, then scratched his beak.

"Strong emotions don't mean romantic interest."

"Interesting."

"What's interesting?"

"Something you said about measuring emotions on the beach. If there was a way to capture the intensity of emotions, then it would make interpretation of people much simpler."

"Do people need to be measured like that?"

"Everything can be measured," Ig said with finality. "Like paint."

"Paint?" Keeping up with Ig's train of thought was giving her a headache.

Ig nodded, put down his plate of half-eaten crumpet and gestured to a machine in the corner. He placed a shell into a large brass bowl and turned a handle which spun interconnected cogs attached to a pestle made of polished wood.

In a matter of moments, the shell became a fine lilac powder. Ig ground more shells into the raw pigment, mixing it with the slime for greater vibrancy. The tylluan grew lost in his work and Crimson felt surplus to requirements, so she left him to it, heading back for her shop with Smudge at her heels.

There was still so much to do. Cleaning the outside for a start and sorting the small courtyard garden. She shuddered. And the privy. And once Ig had all the pigments, then painting. And then, finally, she would be able to create some merchandise for her shop.

Humming with happiness at the thought that the end was in

sight, she arrived back at her shop.

Crimson ran over to the bright red flowers set in a vase on the counter and breathed in the sweet scent. Their petals floated like draped velvet, turning from poppy red at the fringes to a deep burgundy in the centre where tiny yellow stamen drooped with pollen.

Colour. Fabulous, marvellous colour. So, it did exist in this vale outside of the fabrics they sold. She inhaled again. Their scent was sweet, almost vanilla, but faint.

"Where did these come from?" she whispered, a smile plucking at her lips. Maybe she had a secret admirer.

"The forest." Lief's voice made her jump. She hadn't seen the hulking man where he skulked in the shadows.

"You got them?" Her breath stopped. She couldn't believe it. Crimson traced her finger over a delicate petal, admiring the thin veins of dark red that linked the middle to the outer edges. Why would Lief bring her flowers?

"You moaned there was no colour here. I had to show you that you were wrong; there's plenty of colour, if you know where to look."

Crimson smiled. "You can't fool me. You did a nice thing."

Ig was wrong about there being a spark of romance between them, but maybe they could be friends.

He shook his head. "I just didn't want to hear you moaning all the time. It's exhausting and I'm working here, so I have to listen to it all day."

She bit her lip. Now she would have to do something nice

for him. "Leave me your trousers."

"You want me to take my trews off?" He raised an eyebrow.

Crimson blushed. "No! I mean, I'll patch them for you. If you want. As a thank you for the flowers and your work."

"They don't need patching."

Crimson raised an eyebrow. "You'll have a hole in them by the end of the week. See how it's wearing around the thighs?"

"You've been looking at my thighs?"

"No! Oh, forget it." She grabbed the cleaning supplies and swept past, making sure to hit him on the arm with a duster. Of course, she hadn't noticed his legs. Even if there were muscular and well formed. Not that she had noticed, because she hadn't looked at his legs. She wanted to do a nice thing, and he'd thrown it back in her face.

Maybe Ig was right. Maybe there should be a set of rules for interacting with people with no room to mess things up. She sighed. Maybe logic was the way forward.

Chapter 21

~ *Cheeses roll downhill* ~

SUMMER CAME TO SAFFRON Vale, and with it came hotter days, brighter flowers, and the traditional summer activity of cheese rolling.

The residents of this vale appeared to take it very seriously. Crimson watched people stretch and limber up, running on the spot and practicing throwing their heavy rounds of cheese before they climbed the hill to the starting line.

She sat next to Ig on her cloak, which served as a blanket in the heat. Smudge chased after the emerald grasshoppers that leapt through the unmown grass. Now that summer was here, the vibrant colours the vale was famed for shone in the vibrant meadow flowers and verdant greens of the fields that ranged from peppermint to darkest asparagus as the grasses swayed in the slight breeze. In the distance, a sheep bleated. The tylluan had brought a small cart which he set up under a canvas tent. When she'd asked what it was, he'd replied "Medical supplies," in a stiff voice.

Crimson studied the hill, converting the sage green grass into fabric in her mind before sucking in a sharp breath. "That's got to be a forty-degree incline." No wonder her calves ached from the walk up.

"Forty-five if you want to be exact. I measured it." Ig laid out another bandage.

Ovelia joined them with her father, the owner of Eggselsior. The dwarf introduced himself as Pollonius before rubbing his hands together. "Any odds on this year's race?"

Ig shook his head. "The Big Cheddar's going to be strict this year. The maire won't stand for another cheese-based concussion."

"Who's the Big Cheddar?" Crimson asked.

"The great grandson of Jollivity Cheddar himself."

"Saffron Vale boy," Pollonius added.

At Crimson's blank look, Ig expanded. "His record for the largest hard cheese ever rolled downhill still stands. The family is still in the cheese business and one of the Cheddars is the principal judge each year."

"If you won't take my bet, I'll find someone else." Pollonius turned to Crimson. "What about you? Do you fancy a wager?"

Crimson looked around. "It seems unfair, you know all the contestants and who won last year."

Ovelia's father let out a hearty laugh. "Oh no, I don't bet on who catches the cheese. I'm talking about the number of injuries."

"But that's horrible."

He shrugged and clapped her on the shoulder. "It's all in good fun, lass. Can't take yourself too seriously." The dwarf pushed himself to his feet and headed for someone Crimson recognised from the Drunken Gull.

Greezi, the owner of Hambrosia, walked past, heading for the starting line with Hamlet in her wake. Ovelia gave him a small wave, and he smiled back. Tragic, thought Crimson, that they couldn't acknowledge their love for each other.

"I thought I could smell bacon," the dwarf called loud enough to make sure she heard. "Not taking part at your age, are you, orc?"

The orc smiled. "Hiding in the first aid tent, as usual, I see. Let the real cheesers take part."

Hamlet rolled his eyes behind his mother's back.

The dwarf's face turned red behind his bushy beard. "You know I can't run after the great race of 605."

"Well then I guess we know who won't win."

"Nonsense. Ovelia will carry the family name onto the cheese field, won't you lass?"

"Dad!"

Greezi looked the young dwarf up and down. "That slip of a girl hasn't got a chance." With that, she stalked off. Hamlet gave a small shrug of apology and Ovelia shot him a wry smile before her dad took her to one side to talk tactics.

"Do people really get hurt?"

Ig nodded. "I have mentioned that we might select a different hill, one with a gentler incline, but the maire insists on tradition."

With that, there was a sharp whistle from a rotund dwarf with ruddy cheeks who stood on a humongous round of brown-rinded cheddar at the starting line. And the cheese rolling began.

Each contestant launched their own cheese round down the hill, vying for the smoothest and steepest routes down. This meant that many of the rounds crossed each other in organised chaos, which soon descended into full-blown chaos as the participants chased after their cheeses.

The cacophony of shouting from both cheese chasers and spectators drowned out specific cries and expletives, which was just as well because the entire town had turned out to watch, including many children who cheered on, eyes glistening with anticipation for a crash.

They were not disappointed. A few seconds after the race started, Greezi collided with a young man and both fell to the ground in a tumble of elbows and knees, cheeses forgotten. A steward raced over, blew a whistle and had stern words before disqualifying both of them for fighting on the cheese hill.

There were more collisions and several fouls when contestants applied a swift boot to their own rounds to speed it up. The most controversial play was by an older gentleman who the Big Cheddar himself caught kicking another contestant's cheese round, resulting in instant disqualification. The man insisted he had thought it was his, but the judge's decision was final, and the disqualified participant threw his hat on the ground in frustration.

Crimson couldn't tell who'd won as a crowd of cheese chasers crossed the finish line at the same time, but the Big Cheddar had no such problem and announced Gruff, the owner of the Drunken Gull as the winner.

This was the first of many cheese races this year. And the first of many people's trips to the first aid tent where Crimson helped Ig by handing him bandages and dabbing soaked sponges on cuts as people limped in.

She was too busy to notice Lief in the queue until he stepped in front of her and presented a swollen lip for inspection.

"How are you finding your first cheese rolling, Red?" he asked as she pressed a cloth to his face to clear away the blood.

"I've never seen anything like it," Crimson replied.

Lief's lips pulled up into a half smile. "I bet. Who's your money on?"

"I'm not gambling on how many of you get injured. What is wrong with this town?" Her eyes narrowed. "And what makes you think I'm not taking part in the chase?"

He laughed. "You're not serious."

She wasn't, but his outright dismissal that she could take part rankled.

"I'll give you a tip; cheeses roll downhill." With another laugh, he left to watch the children's race as the call went up for baby cheese competitors to make their way to the starting line.

The first aid tent emptied and Ig sighed. "Not too bad. For the first race. It's the big wheel that causes the most casualties." His gaze caught on something and he pointed to a patch of reddish orange above them, about halfway up the only mountain in the vale. "Look – the poppies."

"Poppies?"

"Saffron poppies, I'm sure of it. The only pigment I don't possess. It makes the most vivid red. If only I didn't have to stay here for the injuries."

"They'll be there tomorrow."

Ig shook his head and gave a wistful hoot. "No, they only last a day. I shall have to remember their position for next year."

"I'll go," Crimson said.

Chapter 22

~ Chasing the cheddar ~

CRIMSON SWEATED AS SHE tramped up the mountain. The route was steeper than she'd thought, with slippery shingles that shifted underfoot with every step.

She paused to catch her breath and wipe the moisture from her brow, looking down on the cheese rolling far below. A ting of regret passed through her. She would have loved to stay and watch it all, taking part in the first real town festival since she'd arrived, enjoying the atmosphere of togetherness that she normally experienced during the season of Winter's Tide.

Crimson frowned. Not that she'd felt close with her adopted family last Lantern Night. What was normally a lovely midwinter celebration of hope had turned sour after her fellow apprentice and friend had discarded her like a rag to claim a spot at the guild. Best not to dwell on that.

She squinted, trying to make out familiar forms on the hill, longing to be with them. But it made sense for her to go. Ig was busy tending to injuries, and she had nothing else to do but watch the races and lend a hand. Still, it was a shame to miss such an exhilarating event.

A flash of purple near the white of the tent made her smile as she pictured Smudge darting after damsel flies. From this distance, everyone resembled small blobs of colour, as if she peered into another realm where everyone was tiny.

Crimson's thoughts drifted to her mother. She didn't know much about her, except she was a teg, a dressmaker and had the most beautiful laugh like an enchanting melody that never ceased to bring joy. Her mum would have liked Saffron Vale, she decided. Not that Crimson could ask her.

A familiar dull anger and ache of regret settled in her bones. Every time Crimson thought she had come to terms with her mother's death, it reared up again as a tear in the fabric of her soul. It wasn't fair. She was alone. Why did her mother have to leave her when she was so young?

Crimson shook her head and continued, blinking back tears as she focused on all the blessings in her life, patching over the hole of her mother's loss again. Best to push it back down and focus on the task at hand.

The poppies.

Crimson trudged on, her head down against the chill wind that blew this high even on this warm summer's day. A mountain goat with a trailing coat of fine curly fleece hopped out of her path, sending a flurry of shingles down the mountainside.

As she climbed higher, up ever narrowing and steeper paths, her breath came in short pants and her head filled with cotton.

A huge sheep blocked her way, stamping its foot and swaying its horned head with menace glinting from its dark eyes. Its fleece was enormous; thick wool matted with years of growth. It moved towards her, and she caught the slight limp in its foreleg.

The poor thing. There was a large bramble wound around its leg and caught in its fleece.

"There, there, will you let me help you?" Crimson spoke in her softest voice.

The sheep narrowed its eyes, but stayed still, its injured leg raised off the ground.

Crimson took a deep breath. Taking her fabric scissors from her satchel, she reached forward and snipped the lock of fleece with the bramble attached. The sheep snorted but didn't move.

"OK, and now we unwind…" Crimson moved fast, her deft fingers unlooping the thorny branch from around its leg. "There now."

She stood back and flung the bramble off the path. The sheep tested its weight on its leg and gave a bleat that might have been a thank you before it lowered its head and bared its teeth.

Crimson stepped around it, choosing to scale a rock rather than confront the monster sheep. So much for doing a good deed. Now she was stuck clambering over a boulder.

When she looked down onto the path, the massive creature had gone, leaving her to wonder if she'd imagined it.

A flash of orange caught her eye. The poppies.

Crimson hurried the last few yards and sank to her knees in front of the rare blooms. From afar, they had appeared as a splash of orangey-red on the grey of the mountainside, but up close, they danced in an array of colours from deepest scarlet to dandelion orange. Each blossom was as large as her face. Huge petals flittered as the wind caught them, waving around the deep red of the centre where bees the size of small birds buzzed lazily.

She inhaled their scent; sweet, clean and fresh like the mountain air. A calm fell over her. Maybe she could lay here for a little while and rest. She had come so far, walked for hours. The cheese rolling would finish soon, so there was no reason to hurry back.

Crimson lay on her back, watching the cornflower blue sky through the poppy petals. Somewhere overhead a red kite keened and a throaty baa sounded. Perfect rustic idyll. This was why she had left the city. The calm and peace of the countryside. She should enjoy it. Her eyes closed.

A damp nose pressed against her ear, followed by a snort.

"Smudge, no. It's not morning," Crimson mumbled.

The snorter was insistent.

"Is it really worth risking your life for a brighter shade?" A voice sounded in her head. It sounded a lot like the smug tones of Lief. But that was impossible.

"Yes," Crimson huffed, keeping her eyes closed. "It's a colour to dye for." *Mwhahaha.*

Perhaps she had gone mad from lack of oxygen, but she wasn't that far up, was she? She'd only walked for a couple of hours at most, hadn't she? Or maybe this was all a dream. But she had to get this plant for Ig. She had promised. And he had promised her a shop that people could see for miles, the brightest paint in the queendom.

Which meant she needed to wake up.

She opened her eyes. And stared straight into the scarred face of the gigantic sheep. This was not the sort of face Crimson wanted to see close up in the first moment of waking. Adrenaline spiked through her. She screamed.

The sheep screamed back in the way that only an ovine can and slunk off back to wherever it had come from.

Crimson berated herself. She had been asleep for – she checked the position of the sun in the sky – it looked like she had only been asleep for a few minutes. Best to get the poppies and get back.

As she picked the flowers, and some seed heads for Ig, she yawned, unable to stifle the sleepiness that swept over her. Funny, she felt so drowsy again. Her fuzzy mind focused on the flowers in her hand.

The poppies.

Crimson stuffed them petal first into her bag and her mind cleared. Hoping that the satchel wouldn't damage them too much, she headed back down the mountain. As she passed the bramble she had cut, Crimson saw the sheep stood on the same boulder it had forced her to climb, staring down with unblinking eyes. She hurried on. It had saved her. She had no doubt of that. But it was still a wild animal who made the mountain its home, and she was a trespasser here.

As she reached the part of the mountain that flattened into the top of the cheese rolling hill, Crimson tripped over her skirt. Stumbling, she raced on, hoping to outrun her fall and bracing for the inevitable collision with the line of people standing at the top of the hill. Standing in a line. As if they were ready to run.

The cheese race.

A single humongous round of cheddar rolled down the hill. A whistle blew. The racers sprinted off. Crimson followed, unable to stop her momentum as the hill sloped down.

All she could focus on was staying upright and avoiding crashing into the others who streaked ahead.

And then a blur of purple dodged past the cheese and through the feet of the racers, who stumbled and tripped into a pile of limbs and curse words.

"Smudge, no!" Crimson called with what breath she had left.

The small dragon jumped up, and she lost her balance, rolling onto the trodden down grass. And still, she couldn't stop. She rolled down, bumping over uneven ground and hidden stones with Smudge snorting at her feet until she came to a stop at the bottom of the hill.

Crimson's head swam.

"Unorthodox, I grant you, but there's nothing in the rules to stop wild animals getting onto the green."

She looked up to see the Big Cheddar himself staring down at her.

"Sorry," she whispered.

"I told you; dragons are wild. They're not pets," Lief said.

"We have a winner!" The head judge announced.

For one awful moment, Crimson thought it was her. But he walked over to Greezi and held her arm up high.

A huge cheer went up from everyone except the contestants that Smudge had felled, who glared Crimson's way with ominous mutterings that she hadn't even signed the disclaimer and shouldn't have been allowed on the hill.

Greezi grinned round and hefted the gigantic wheel of cheese above her head. There wasn't a dent in the wrinkled crust.

"To fondue!" the orc yelled.

A bigger cheer rang around the field and the stronger members of the community lifted Greezi up and took her over to the food tent where Milus the blacksmith tended a fire with his good hand, keeping his metal hand away from the flames.

Crimson limped over to the abandoned first aid tent.

Smudge fussed around her. "At least you're happy to see me."

In response, the dragon rolled over so she could stroke his belly.

"But I need to make you a harness, so you don't get into more trouble." Crimson's brow furrowed as she laid out the pattern pieces in her mind, estimating how much ribbon she might need and whether fabric would be strong enough for a determined dragon.

A shadow fell over her. She squinted up and sighed as she recognised Lief's muscular shadow.

"What do you want?"

"Is that any way to talk to someone who's brought you food?"

Stitches. Now she would have to apologise to him for being rude. And she wasn't in the mood. Instead, she mumbled her thanks and took a plate filled with bread and apples from him. Crimson lifted a chunk of bread to her lips.

"Ah-ah," Lief said, wagging his finger as he sank to the ground next to her in a fluid motion. "Here."

He placed a pottery bowl of thick melted cheese in between them. Crimson eyed it with suspicion.

"Worried I've poisoned it?" he joked. With an exaggerated motion, Lief dipped his own bread in it before popping the whole piece in his mouth. He leaned back, supporting himself with his arm, and closed his eyes as he relished the fondue.

Crimson followed his example and dipped a small piece of crusty bread into the fondue. The gooey cheese clung to the bread, coating it in a thick layer of rich sauce. She sniffed. Sharp and salty with a tang of apple. Crimson placed it in her mouth and let out a moan of satisfaction. This was good fondue.

"Did you really come here to share fondue with me?" she asked after they had consumed half of the bowl in silence.

Lief shifted on the ground. He glanced down to where Smudge lay with his head in Crimson's lap.

"You want to berate me about Smudge's behaviour? I already feel awful about that." She rested her hand on the dragon's head.

"It's not your fault. He's not a pet." Lief kept going over Crimson's protest. "And it's not his fault, either. He's a wild animal. He doesn't belong in a town."

"He's friendly. He likes being around people."

"He's a coastal dragon. He'd like it more if he was with his own kind. Animals need to know where they belong. They need a pack, or they end up alone and miserable."

"Like you?" It was a cheap jibe, and a half-hearted one.

Lief said nothing, instead he looked across the fields for a long time and Crimson had the feeling that maybe he wasn't just talking about the dragon. He let out a sigh. "Do you really want to be responsible if he accidentally burns down the town?"

Crimson scratched Smudge's spikes and he let out a purr of contentment. He was her closest friend here in Saffron Vale, choosing to be with her from her first night in the vale. But she couldn't deny he had caused chaos today. And he had only run across a field. Smudge could breathe fire; she knew that much. Did she really expect him to live in a flammable building? More flammable once she had fabric and stock in the shop. A mistimed sneeze could destroy everything.

"And, is there somewhere nearby, with other dragons?"

"Wyrm Rock. Off the coast. It's a dragon sanctuary, protected by the crown and reserved for dragons and other wildlife that chooses to make its home there."

"You've been there?"

"It's under my protection as warden."

"Would Smudge like it there?"

"I'm sure he'd love it."

Crimson peered deep into his eyes, gauging his honesty. He believed what he said. She was sure of that much. Maybe it was for the best. Wardens knew what they were talking about when it came to nature after all, it was in the job description; they protected forests and apparently dragon rocks too.

Smudge snorted. Was he telling her he wanted to go?

"Alright."

"Glad you've seen sense."

"But not until his wing's better."

Chapter 23

~ *Painting is a messy business* ~

IG DELIVERED ON HIS promise of bright paints several days later when he showed up with huge tins in every colour of the rainbow. Crimson squealed with delight and even did a little jig, which caused Lief to smile, which she ignored.

"And there I thought you were nearly done with me," he laughed as Crimson grabbed Ig's arm and twirled him round.

She ignored him. Not even Lief's jibes could destroy her good mood. She used a screwdriver to prise the lid off of a tin and sighed at the swirl of colour.

Smudge sniffed it and sneezed a small fireball onto the dew wet grass that grew up between the cobblestones outside the shop. That was one way to weed, Crimson thought, as it sizzled and shrivelled up to a charred clump.

"It's one coat. Four hours drying time. You'll need to stir it before you start," Ig said, demonstrating with a stick.

Crimson tied up her hair with the bright saffron sunshine ribbon she loved and grabbed a paintbrush.

"If you're starting, I'll head off," Ig said with a wave.

"You're leaving?"

"Much to do and I can't abide paint in my feathers." He ruffled his tawny feathers to emphasise the point and left Crimson and Lief to it.

"I'll do downstairs, you do upstairs," Crimson said, her head already swimming with ideas for decorating the walls.

Lief grunted his agreement and walked upstairs with a couple of tins of paint in his large hands.

Crimson sighed. She was so close. After today, she would have a shop that she could fill with her creations. Her fingers itched for her sewing needle. But that would have to wait until after the paint was dry.

She selected a paintbrush and began slopping plain white onto the walls as a base coat while she daydreamed about the finished look. She could choose a different colour for every wall, but there were so many colours…and she could mix them together to make endless shades. Too much choice.

"What are you doing?"

Crimson stopped, paintbrush in hand, paint dripping onto the floor. "Painting." Was Lief deliberately obtuse?

"First, you want to put down a dust sheet to stop paint staining the boards."

"Oh."

She balanced her brush on the tin and helped him spread out a large canvas sheet.

"And second, that's not how you paint."

Crimson folded her arms. "What are you talking about?"

"That small brush is for edging. When you do the large surface, use a bigger brush like this. Long, even strokes." He demonstrated with the white paint before offering her the brush.

Crimson took it and copied him.

Lief moved behind her and placed his hand over hers, guiding her strokes. His body was warm against hers and Crimson felt a heat growing in her stomach and blossoming over her face. Just as it got too much, and she felt she had to duck away, he stepped back.

"Better, Red."

"My name is Crimson." She retreated into the more comfortable emotion of frustrated anger and frowned up at him.

Lief smiled down, grabbed another tin of paint and headed upstairs. "And don't overload the brush," he called down.

"Stitches to him," she said, but a smile pulled at her lips. Somehow, even though he was awful, she enjoyed their verbal sparring and sometimes she was almost sure there was something more. But he'd made it clear he didn't want her friendship. Stitches. People were confusing. Maybe she should take a leaf out of Ig's book and get a formula for dealing with people.

***

Four hours later and the paint had dried. Ig had worked a minor miracle with the formula. Crimson was spattered with flecks of white paint, Smudge's nose was smeared with white after he'd knocked over a brush – thank goodness Lief had insisted on a dust sheet – and Lief's hair sported a thin coating of white spots so it looked like he had gone grey in a morning.

"Working with you has aged me," he had quipped when she commented on his new look.

Now, they surveyed the downstairs.

"What colour are you thinking?" Lief asked.

"There's too many to choose from. Maybe I could paint each half wall a different colour, then the counter in a yellow."

Lief winced. "That's a lot of colour."

"That's what my clothes are about. The joy of colour, combining them in unexpected ways, it's what I love. I want people to smile when they see my designs in their wardrobes. I want my creations to bring happiness to the everyday." Crimson's face shone with passion as she described her vision out loud for the first time.

"So, you're filling this space with bright clothes?"

"That's what I said, isn't it?" Wasn't he listening? Sometimes she wanted to stamp her foot in frustration with this man.

"Don't you want your clothes to stand out?"

Crimson frowned.

"If the walls are painted with colour, then the clothes will be lost."

"I suppose…but it's just …dull ."

Lief stood and paced the shop. "What if we painted the counter in your favourite colour? Or the same colour as your name? And then, over here, we could do a rainbow. That would brighten the place up but not detract from your display, which you could have here."

Crimson twirled in the centre of the shop, picturing it. "Yes," she breathed. It was perfect. "Where did you learn so much about interior design?"

Lief shrugged. "Seemed obvious." His expression shuttered. He was back to his closed self. But Crimson didn't care, she was too caught up in his vision.

"I'll sketch out the rainbow, can you do the counter?"

"What colour?"

"Sunshine yellow. That will go with the rainbow."

"And there's something else I've been thinking about." Crimson chewed her lip, thinking how best to put the saffron poppy paint to use. Ig had outdone himself and there were several tins of the glorious rich colour. "What do you think about painting the outside of the shop?"

"I think it's the sort of crazy thing you'd do, Red. But if you want it to be a surprise for the big opening, best to do it at night."

"How will I see?"

"Leave it to me. I've got excellent night vision."

Crimson's brow wrinkled. Who could see in the dark well enough to paint a shop?

***

CRIMSON STRETCHED AND ROLLED her shoulders, working out a kink in her muscles. Her painting hand and arm were sore, but the shop was finished; a bright, airy space where she could showcase her wares. The kitchen was a cheery yellow with dark blue cupboards and the only space she hadn't seen was the upstairs.

"I could use a bath," she said.

Lief sniffed and agreed.

"Hey, you don't smell like a bed of roses." She nudged him with her shoulder, then sighed. "I wish there was a bathhouse here."

"We use the hot springs."

"That sounds amazing. Will you take me?"

Lief looked up, then down, then huffed. "Fine."

"Come on, Smudge, we're going to the springs."

Chapter 24

~ Hot Springs ~

THE HOT SPRINGS, LIKE much of Saffron Vale, didn't look like much at first glance. Lief had led them to the forest and, after a brief stop at his cabin for towels, had followed a path out behind his house to a clearing where dirty turquoise water bubbled up in large pools below a steaming waterfall that trickled into the largest pool.

A series of smaller, interconnected pools carved into the rock by years of erosion fed from the larger one and the water flowed out, following a small brook that she thought went to join the Rainbow River further downstream.

The smell that clung to the clearing was what one might describe as bad eggs, although some people may use a less polite word for the pong of sulphurous mineral steam that hung in wispy tendrils, lending the glade a sense of otherworldliness.

Smudge bounded over and plunged into the nearest pool with a splash. His little legs paddled hard, and he dived under. When he reemerged, he shook his head, sending hot droplets of water everywhere.

Crimson laughed and held up her hands against the spray.

Dislodged by the water, Smudge's bandage floated away to the other side.

Encouraged by the dragon, Crimson asked, "Where do we get changed?"

Lief laughed and pulled off his paint-spattered shirt. "This isn't the city, Red. No fancy changing rooms or servers to offer you iced tea while you relax."

Crimson turned away. She should go back home. Maybe come later on when no one was around. A swoosh of water told her that Lief had entered the pool. Time to go.

Except… she was here now and the thought of a bath and getting clean was so appealing. Up until the kitchen sink was fixed, she'd had to make do with a small bowl of cold water filled from the communal pump. And, although she'd upgraded to warm water from the kettle now the kitchen was no longer out of bounds, it wasn't the same as immersing herself in glorious hot water and getting 'properly clean' as her adopted aunt, Marie, would say.

She draped the towel around her body and attempted to get undressed with one hand while the other held up the towel to protect her modesty.

"What are you doing?"

"Getting changed."

"I won't look."

"No offense, but I don't trust you."

"In what world is that not offensive?"

Crimson didn't bother to reply. She managed to tug off her dress and then slipped into a pool on the other side of the clearing. It was the perfect temperature, and the heat sank into her body, warming her to her core.

"Are you still wearing your underclothes?"

Crimson fought with the flimsy fabric that now floated around her in the pool, rising up with the flow of the water. "I thought you said you wouldn't look."

"Is that how they get washed in the city?"

"It's common decency. You can't expect people to get naked in a shared gender space."

"Seems unhygienic to me." Lief disappeared under the water and reappeared with his hair plastered to his face.

He reached out of the pool and Crimson averted her gaze and focused on the billowing linen of her underdress. If she scrunched it up and sat on it, she could stop it floating in front of her. A loud pop from behind her caused her to flush from embarrassment, while Lief chuckled. A bubble had built up, trapped by the fabric, only to release in one loud, wet splosh.

"Here." Lief chucked her a bar of soap.

Crimson caught it, the slippery block sliding between her fingers before she had a firm grip. The lavender fresh scent was a welcome relief from the gone-off eggy tang from the springs. She scrubbed her body underneath her shift, much to Lief's amusement, and then lay in the pool, her eyes closed as the tension and stress flowed out of her muscles.

This was better than the tin bath at Guilder Senda's home and better than the communal steam rooms she'd visited with her friend Ayla in Oasis. This was bliss.

In the trees surrounding them, birds sang a cheerful tune. Her lips curved into a smile as she allowed her spirit to soar with their glorious song. There must be magic in the air because even the worry about her shop had dimmed to the tiniest flicker instead of the stamping giant it had become in her mind.

Everything would be alright. Everything would work out. She had space to work and once the town saw her creations, they would embrace her as one of their own and she would be hailed as a success across the queendom. She sighed and sank deeper into the water.

"The dragon's wing is better." Lief's voice jarred her back to reality.

Crimson peered at Smudge, who jumped from rock to rock before diving into the pool again with the joyful abandon of an animal who loved water and heat and had no care in the world. As if to prove Lief's point, Smudge spread his wings and glided a few feet.

"Maybe…"

"I really think it's for the best if he goes back to the wild."

"Hmmm."

"We could go to Wyrm Rock tomorrow if you like. And if Smudge doesn't like it, he'll make his way back here. After all, he got here before."

Crimson nodded, the magic of the springs wearing down her resistance. If Smudge was healed, maybe it was best for him to live with other dragons. She didn't want to hold him back.

They stayed in the springs until the sky began to darken and Crimson's skin was wrinkled from the hot water.

Getting out was another exercise in embarrassment for Crimson and amusement for Lief. She stood shivering in her wet, and almost see through, linen shift as she puzzled out what to do. If she removed her shift, she would be naked, which she didn't want. But if she kept it on and slipped her dress over the top, she'd end up soaking her dress and probably freeze on the way back to her shop.

With a laugh, Lief announced he would stand behind a large tree until she was ready. She muttered a thank you between chattering teeth and, keeping her eyes on the tree, got dried and dressed in record time. She wrung out her sodden shift and folded it to better avoid creases before telling Lief it was safe.

They parted ways at his cabin. Crimson was confident she could follow the path back to town. At her feet, Smudge worried at the bandage she'd reapplied to his wing, just in case.

"Thank you," Crimson said. "For everything. The shop. The

springs. Everything."

Lief gave her a genuine smile that softened his hard face. "Not a problem, Red. And I'll see you tomorrow for our trip."

She nodded and drifted home in a cloud of happy relaxation with Smudge at her side, also moving in a sluggish manner.

As she headed upstairs to curl up on the floor – she still hadn't got a bed – she froze.

Lief had painted the room white as she'd asked, perfect for working as it would bounce any light around, brightening the room. But one wall was a rich red. As she studied it, she realised it wasn't any shade of red. It was crimson. Like her name.

It gave the room a touch of coziness and welcomed her into the space, reminding her that this was her bedroom, not just a workshop. It was a thoughtful touch, and she reached out to touch the wall, marvelling at the shade he must have mixed to make Ig's red less brash.

And the thought that she would see him tomorrow sent her off into a happy slumber filled with warm dreams.

Chapter 25

~ Wyrm Rock ~

"ARE YOU READY?" LIEF asked.

Crimson nodded, not trusting herself to speak. She climbed into the faded blue boat, took a seat at the back and called Smudge, who jumped in with ease, flexing his healed wing as if to emphasise that he was good as new.

Lief untied the thick rope that secured the rowing boat to the jetty and got in after them, looping the rope in a neat pile under a seat. He sat on the bench in the middle of the boat, his back facing the prow, and unhooked the oars.

"Don't you need to see where you're going?" Crimson asked, unsure if this was some sort of joke to make her feel better. Although why Lief would try to cheer her up was a mystery.

"You row backwards. Like this." With two quick pulls on the oars, they were away from land and heading out to sea.

"What if you hit something?"

Lief laughed. "We're in the ocean. What am I going to hit?"

"Rocks? Fish? I don't know."

"The lighthouse tells us where the dangerous coast is – over there. And fish know better than to get their heads banged by a boat. But if you see anything you think I need to know, you can tell me."

Crimson stroked Smudge's head as Lief rowed, her fingers tracing his warm scales as if she could commit them to memory. He lapped at her hands with his wet tongue, unaware of the journey's purpose. It was for the best. At least that's what Lief said, and he knew more about wild animals than most, living so close to the woods.

So why did her heart feel like it wanted to explode with sadness? It was the best thing for the creature who shared her home, who she cared about more than she thought she could care about a living thing. And she was so selfish that her only emotions were grief instead of joy that he could be free and live among his own kind.

Crimson pushed her tears back and concentrated on the horizon, knowing that if she looked down into Smudge's trusting amber eyes, she'd collapse and worry the small dragon.

A large black rock loomed in the distance. As Crimson watched, feeling her heart plummet through the base of the boat and down into the depths of the ocean, the rock seemed to twist and move under her gaze. She shuddered. This was a bad idea.

She should tell Lief to turn the boat around and go home. Smudge wouldn't survive out here. His scales would fade from their magnificent sheen to a dull mouldy berry shade, and he would die. A small sob escaped her throat as the scenarios chased each other around her mind, choking her with desolation.

And still they pulled closer, the rhythmic slapping of the oars against the water beating in her ears like a drum marching them to an execution.

Nearer the forbidding island, the sun peeked through the thin clouds and shone its rays onto Wyrm Rock. Crimson realised that the strange undulations she had glimpsed from further away were, in fact, masses of dragons of every size and colour swarmed over the land in a rainbow of shimmering scales. She gasped and this time it was in wonder at the beauty of the dragon colony.

A few dragons detached themselves from a cliff and dived into the glistening azure waves, wings held close against their backs as they plunged beneath the surface.

Crimson leaned over the edge of the boat and shouted. "They've fallen in! We have to help! Over there!"

"Wait," Lief said.

Crimson stared at the rippling waves for long, drawn out moments, holding her own breath as thoughts of dragons drowning scudded across her mind's eye. And then they resurfaced, snouts full of flapping fish as the dragons flew upwards to rejoin the rest of the colony, gulping down the silver fish with a flick of their heads. Others bobbed in the water, swallowing their prizes before diving back into the depths for more fishing.

Smudge placed his front feet on the side, next to Crimson, and strained his neck forward, a pleading note in his growling whine.

Before she could stop him, Smudge jumped out of the boat and landed in the water with a splash.

"No!" Crimson reached after him.

The boat wobbled, tilting dangerously to one side. Smudge disappeared under the sea, his purple scales disappearing into the dark water.

Strong arms grabbed around her waist and tugged her back into the boat. Crimson fell against Lief's chest and struggled to right herself.

"He'll drown!"

"Look."

Crimson stopped squirming and looked where his fingers pointed as Smudge bobbed back to the surface, a small fish in his mouth. With a flap of his wings, he climbed back into the boat and dropped the fish at Crimson's feet.

She laughed in relief, sinking back against Lief. "Clever boy!"

Smudge nosed the flipping fish and nudged it towards them.

Crimson picked it up. The fish slipped through her fingers. Smudge leapt forward and gobbled it up, licking his reptilian lips in satisfaction.

Lief shifted and placed Crimson back on her seat before moving to the rowing bench and taking them to the island.

The closer they got, the more excited Smudge became. The small dragon jumped in and out of the boat so many times that Crimson started bailing water out, the frothy tang of salt singing in her nose as she got into the rhythm of cupping water and sending it over the side.

And then, with a thud, the boat pulled up to the shore. Lief hopped out and pulled the boat up the beach until it rested half in, half out of the sea.

Crimson climbed out, accepting Lief's calloused hand to help her step onto the sand. The cove was quiet and secluded with light sand, almost white in the sun. Towering cliffs sheltered it, scattered with mosses and heathers in shades ranging from dusky orange to rose pink.

As Crimson gazed around the sheltered beach, Lief returned to the boat, bent low, and retrieved a woven wicker basket. With a sly smile, he walked back to where Crimson stood and brandished the basket.

"A spot of lunch?"

Crimson's eyes widened at his thoughtfulness. "But where will we sit? The rocks all have barnacles on them."

Lief opened the basket and unfurled a blanket. As he attempted to lay it flat on the sand, a gust of wind tugged the far edge, sending it flying into his face. Crimson bit back a laugh and hurried to help, telling herself that the squirming in her stomach was the tail end of sea sickness and nothing to do with the boyish grin on Lief's face.

She gripped the thick cloth and between them, they spread out the blanket. Crimson plonked herself at one end to stop it flying away again. The wool was rough spun but so felted with use that it barely prickled where it touched her bare skin. She traced the pattern with her gaze. It was a simple tartan woven with rustic yellows, oranges and browns; all the hues of the coming season of autumn.

Crimson glanced up at Lief. It fit in with what she knew of him. Everything practical and with purpose yet well made. She could tell this blanket was well-loved and years old and yet it lasted and was comfier today with its trodden knap than the rough wool had been when it was first made. A perfect picnic blanket.

"We make a good team," Lief said as he sat at the other end and unloaded the basket, spreading cold pasties and boiled eggs alongside scones ready made with medlar jelly sandwiched between their golden halves and thick slices of yeasty yellow saffron cake, the speciality of the vale.

"We do?" Crimson's heart fluttered.

"The blanket."

Of course, that was what he meant. Nothing more. He offered her a pasty and Crimson took it without meeting his gaze, half expecting a trick, for him to push her flat on her face even though he had never done anything quite so cruel.

There was a distance he kept that set her on edge and a mocking tone he used that made her rile back against him with minimal provocation. But he kept his hand steady as she took the pasty, and she eyed him as she chewed on the thick crust and succulent meaty interior, wondering if this trip was a truce of some kind.

Perhaps the cheese rolling had shown she wasn't so much of an uppity outsider as he feared. And for her part, it was hard to hold at a distance someone who was so keen to help he had rowed her to an island for her beloved Smudge.

She broke off half her pasty and gave it to her pet. The dragon took it and chomped down, spreading crumbs all over the tartan rug. Crimson laughed and Smudge curled into a sleeping ball as they ate in silence, permeated only by flapping wings of dragons overhead and the occasional screech of a gull.

After eating, Crimson left Smudge to nap and explored the cove. At the very edges were slippery rock pools where striped hermit crabs cavorted among trails of dark seaweed.

A tiny dragon, no larger than her palm, darted across the slate grey rocks to investigate her. Crimson held her hand flat, and it ran onto her skin, its tiny claws hard on her hand. It stayed there for a long moment while Crimson held her breath before it ran off to chase a sand fly that hopped over the rock pool.

"This is a magical place."

"It is."

Crimson jumped. She hadn't heard Lief approach, and his voice was low and soft by her ear.

Her gasp of shock turned into something closer to a giggle.

"Smudge will be happy here," he said.

Maybe Lief was right. Her gaze tracked Smudge to where he stretched and wandered over to a rock where a couple of dragons of similar size rested. They watched him approach with lazy flicks of their tails, sending sapphire flashes of light onto the rocks as their scales caught the sun.

He jumped up, ready to play. The larger of the two pretended to ignore him before flying down to the ground and dipping low in a play posture. Smudge copied the gesture, and the two dragons ran around in circles.

Crimson gasped as a lick of flame came from Smudge's playmate, but her dragon ducked out of the way and sent his own burst of fire back with a playful snort.

"He can't get that in Woolton." Lief had moved closer, and the heat of his arm radiated through Crimson's sleeve.

She sighed. No, Smudge could never have this sort of interaction in the confines of the town. Her lips curved at his obvious enjoyment. And, as if to disprove all her worries, Smudge followed the larger dragon into the waves and emerged with a wiggling fish, which he devoured in two bites. He could feed himself.

Crimson watched as the two dragons worried a large crab they'd found by a brownish rock. The crab snapped its pincers and held them off until it dug itself deep into the sand.

She nodded. This was Smudge's natural environment, and he would thrive here. It was her own selfishness that wanted him at her side, snuggled up warm together as the evenings drew in. But still, she lingered.

Smudge bounded over to them, his tongue flapping with joy and she bent to stroke his scales just the way he liked; a tickle under the chin combined with a scratch by his horns. He snorted with pleasure before running off to join his new friend.

Lief nudged her. "We should go."

She nodded, a heavy lump stuck in her throat as she folded the blanket and stepped back into the boat. Lief stayed quiet as he pushed them out deep enough that he could row.

Smudge didn't even notice them leave, too busy exploring the cove. When they were so far out that she could barely see him, Crimson stood and called out, leaning over the side of the boat until it dipped low in the water, certain that this was the wrong thing. She hadn't even said a proper goodbye. There was no way the tiny dragon could survive on his own.

The wind dragged her anguished cry away.

Lief set the oars and gathered her in his arms. "It's for the best."

She took some comfort from his warm surrounding presence, so confident and calm.

"Nothing that feels this bad can be for the best. We have to go back."

He shook his head, the stubble on his chin catching her hair. "If he wants to come back, he will."

Crimson pushed herself out of the embrace and met his gaze, pleading with her wet eyes.

"I'm not going back."

"Then I'll row." She snatched for an oar, but he caught her hand.

"Don't make it worse."

They stared at each other for a long time as the boat bobbed on the waves, until Crimson looked away.

Biting her lip, she moved back to her seat and hugged her arms around her stomach. She wouldn't take comfort from someone so dead inside that they couldn't understand that she'd made a terrible mistake and had to go back. Just because he wanted to live alone, didn't mean everyone had to.

Crimson squinted at Wyrm Rock as it faded into the horizon, desperate for the flashes of purple that told her Smudge was alive.

"If he really wanted to come with us, he'd have flown out to the boat when we were closer," Lief said.

"Don't talk to me. I hate that I've done this. I hate you for making me do this," Crimson said, her breath hissing out in a harsh whisper. It wasn't fair. But despair had its claws in her and she wanted to lash out, to hurt someone as if that would ease the pain.

Rain began to fall in a soft mizzle that clung to her hair and eyelashes. She was alone now.

Lief said nothing, not rising to her bait. Instead, he nodded and kept rowing.

And Crimson didn't dissolve into tears until she was back home, alone. That had to count for something.

Chapter 26

~ Alone ~

CRIMSON DIDN'T BREAK DOWN the minute she got home. She decided the best way to process the loss of her dragon friend was in the same manner with which she'd processed every loss in her life from her mother to her place with the guild; that is by throwing herself into another project.

When her mother had passed and Guilder Senda had taken her in, she'd focused on learning the craft and becoming worthy of a place in the Dressmakers' Guild. And she'd found an aptitude for sewing and pattern cutting that meant she was sure to get a place, if it hadn't been for the interference of someone she'd thought was a friend and the conservative attitude of Senda himself.

And so, when her dream of joining the guild had dissolved before her, she'd decided to follow the threads that the vales set out for her and come to the place that manufactured the brightest fabrics in the queendom; Saffron Vale. She'd thrown herself into renovating her shop with blood, sweat, and tears. And here she was, the proud owner of her own shop, freshly painted and ready for her creations.

It felt empty. But she pushed down the churning sadness in her stomach and instead ran her hands over the fabric that Hardy had delivered. Of course, her shop was empty. She hadn't made anything yet. Soon it would be full of clothing and accessories, and people would flock to it.

Crimson allowed herself a moment of indulgence, imagining her name spoken in every corner of the Queendom with awe as people asked if a dress was a 'genuine Brouderer'. She waited for the usual heady feeling of her heart soaring in her chest as she daydreamed, but today it remained flat.

Of course, her body recognised how futile her dreams were without work to back them up. Still refusing to acknowledge the pain of loneliness, Crimson's fingers drifted over the pile of fabric. So much choice. Ig had outdone himself with the selection of colours; all vibrant and in every bright shade of the rainbow. And she would have to ask him about the weave, because it was so fine, she could barely make out the different threads.

Bright colours. She needed the brightest colours to banish the blues that fogged her heart and soul. Leaving Smudge was the right thing to do. She had to tell herself that and not imagine him lost and hurt, searching for her on the dark island.

A sound downstairs sent her running to the door. Had he come back?

Crimson flung open the shutters. A fuzz bat chittered and flapped away, looking like a doughnut with wings. Not her dragon, then. Maybe he really was better off on the rock. Maybe now he was with his own kind, he wouldn't spare her a second thought.

Good. That was how it was meant to be. The natural order of things.

So why did it hurt so much?

A flash of white caught her gaze and she swallowed to see a person staring up at her shop. The fuzz bat looped back and hit her in the side of the head with a thud. Crimson blinked away the stars and shooed the bat away, when she looked back, the person was gone. Was it the ghost who had appeared in the storm again? Just her luck to pick a haunted shop in a stupid town where everyone hated her, and she'd lost her dragon to her own stupidity.

Crimson closed the shutters with a click and headed back upstairs to her bedroom slash workroom. The only sure way to distract herself was with work.

She tied her hair back with her yellow ribbon and selected a bright sunshine yellow cloth that matched it and contrasting vivid scarlet for pockets with a lighter linen for the lining. How could someone be sad when they were dressed as sunshine? And maybe it would cheer her up while she worked it into a dress.

Crimson opened her mother's sewing box. Inside were the tools of her trade. Her razor-sharp fabric scissors that never left the box, unlike the emergency pair she carried in her satchel, spools of threads organised like a rainbow and silver pins of all sizes.

She pulled out the vibrant moss green thread that had belonged to her mother. Everything else in the box she had replaced without a second thought, but green had been her mother's favourite colour, representing the vividness of nature, and she had never used up this thread. It was the crocus engraved on the wooden spool that had nudged her to Saffron Vale.

She brought it to her lips. "Oh Mum, I hope I've made the right choice."

Crimson waited, hoping for a sign or a feeling of inner peace, so she would know her decision was the right one. But there was no sign from beyond the grave, no fluttering of the candle flame in its lantern, no faint pat on her cheek.

Tears spilled down her face. It was too much. She had no one. All she had was work.

Wiping her eyes, she set out the familiar patterns and cut out the pieces that would form the dress, making sure she left plenty of room in the hem if she needed to let it out later, depending on who bought it.

She threaded her needle with expert precision and her fingers flew over the fabric, stabbing it with neat stitches in a sort of catharsis. With every puncture of the material,

Crimson repeated her mother's mantra; 'Everything has its time.'

And she added her own; "It will all be alright. Time means it won't hurt anymore." *I won't let myself get close to anyone again.*

With each stitch, she reinforced her motto, imagining that she could sew up her heartache as easily as she could sew fabric. Determination would get her through.

Crimson sewed until the small hours that night and all other nights that sennight, collapsing onto her creations and waking with fabric stuck to her face and pins and needles in her limbs. She ignored any knocks on her door and only ventured out when her hands shook from fatigue and hunger to buy the basics.

Out of spite for herself, she emerged from her wallowing to announce the grand opening with absurdly short notice, forcing herself to work longer hours to get everything done.

Work was the only thing that could numb her feelings, and if it couldn't transform them into happiness, at least it could exhaust her so the pit of loss in her stomach didn't engulf her. And, as time passed and Smudge stayed away, she could convince herself that she had done the right thing.

Chapter 27

~ *The Grand Opening* ~

NERVES FLUTTERED IN CRIMSON'S belly, filling the empty dragon-shaped hole that had sat there for weeks. It might be temporary, but it was a welcome distraction.

All her work meant that her shop was filled with examples of her creations. Some ready to buy with the slightest alterations to suit the purchaser while others were in earlier stages all set for full tailoring. And she had made hair bands and ribbons and small head pieces so none of the precious fabric was wasted and there was something for every size purse.

This place was the culmination of her creative vision. A cacophony of clashing bold colours that exploded into a rainbow of clothing that complimented the bright colours on the walls. Determination mixed with inspiration to rid herself of the churning emptiness that had settled in her chest since Smudge had left.

"It's beautiful," Dilly said, gazing around as she placed a tray of brownies on the counter. "I've never seen anything like it."

"Do you think it's enough?" Crimson replied, straightening a bolt of fabric.

Crimson had decided to distract herself by planning the biggest opening she could, and cakes were just a small part of that. The maire would arrive any minute to cut the crimson ribbon she had selected because it matched her name, and she had booked the town band for the morning and instructed them to play upbeat music.

She ran a finger down her list. Everything had a large tick next to it, marking off the completion of her to do list. Seeing everything completed would normally bring her a sense of satisfaction, but she couldn't shake the sadness that followed her around, dulling her disposition and clouding what should be the happiest day of her life.

A screeching sound, like fingers down a blackboard, had her racing outside. And straight into Lief.

"You." Crimson spat the word. She didn't quite blame him for her decision to abandon Smudge, but he had been part of it, and she was ready for a fight. She welcomed the simmer of rage that flooded her veins. She had pushed it down and channelled her anger into her work, ignoring her heartbreak and hurt, but now it came back tenfold.

"Still here, are you?"

"You're standing outside my shop."

"Can't blame me for wondering. You didn't answer the door when I knocked."

Why would he knock on her door? Crimson shoved the thought aside. "I thought you might take the hint and leave me alone. Now, why are you here?"

Lief raised his fiddle with a smile. "You hired the band, didn't you?"

Stitches. Typical small-town trick that he would be part of it.

"I hoped for some music to serenade my customers, not scare them away."

"Then let us warm up our instruments."

The curl of amusement on his lip as he drew his bow across the strings to make a screeching wail made her want to stamp her feet. She whirled back around to go inside before she gave in to the childish impulse.

And pulled up short to avoid knocking over the maire.

"The fair Miss Brouderer, good morrow to you." He bent to take her hand, and visions of another slobbery kiss on her skin played through her mind. Crimson stuffed her hands into the safety of her pockets. But the maire was not to be denied. He patted her bright pockets, moving into her personal space. "Ah, these must be the pockets I have heard so much about. A clever invention indeed. It makes one wonder what you might hide within."

"Er, they're useful for hiding money purses." The maire winced and withdrew his hand. "Or, in my case, pins. I always seem to find them, and a pocket is the perfect place to store them. I wouldn't want anyone to step on them."

"No. Quite." Maire Bowan sucked his thumb. "Well, shall we get on with it then? Hardy! My ceremonial scissors."

Hardy assembled a folding table and placed a huge red velvet box on it. He undid the clasp and revealed a pair of jewelled scissors almost as tall as the maire. Crimson eyed them with a professional gaze. They were beautiful, but impractical. Not only the size but the placement of the rubies which would press into the palms of anyone using them for a prolonged period of time.

She ran a thumb along her own fabric scissors in her pocket next to her mother's thread. Much better to have a plain, practical pair than something ornate that didn't fit in with her lifestyle.

Maire Bowan hefted them and made a couple of practice swipes, causing Crimson to step back as the blades swished together too close for comfort.

Behind her, the banshee cries of out of tune instruments became actual music, and she found her foot tapping along in time with the beat. Excellent. Now she just needed customers.

The maire stood on a box that Hardy had somehow carried along with the stool and the scissors, stamped his foot and gave a rousing cry of "Oyez!" attracting the attention of everyone walking past. Punctuating his words with waves of the giant scissors, he started his speech.

There was something about welcoming new talent and creativity to the town, but Crimson's heart beat too strong in her ears to listen and giants stamped a jig in her stomach. She clenched her hands in her pockets, smiled and nodded in what she hoped were the right places as the maire spoke about his initiatives to repurpose unusable places.

Her ears perked up as he listed all the problems with the building she had rented. So, he'd known about the woodworm before.

And then Hardy gave a pointed cough and Maire Bowan smiled and brought his speech to an end. "And so it is with great pleasure and no small amount of pride for the protégée I welcomed into this great town, that I pronounce Brouderer's Boutique open!"

To a smattering of applause, he brandished the scissors and cut the ribbon that held up an enormous old sail that Ig had lent her. The tylluan had helped design the ingenious connection of ribbons and rope that fastened the plain sail over the shop and now fluttered to the ground revealing the bright yellow plaster beneath.

A gasp rippled around the townsfolk at the unexpected flush of colour.

Lief, her co-conspirator in the painting, shot her a wink and she nodded to him, her cheeks flushing.

Crimson shared a smile with Ig and mouthed 'thank you'. Ig assured her that the colour would last thanks to a special preservative in the paint that would counteract the harsh wind and rain that assaulted the vale in the winter. And here, in the glorious sunshine, it glowed.

And not only that, there, painted in exquisite detail, were oversized crocus flowers gleaming in the myrrx purple paint. How had they got there? Who had Lief got to paint the flowers in secret? She hadn't seen anyone at the shop apart from him, unless… was he the artist? Crimson's head swam as she drank it in. Her shop. Beautiful and colourful, better than she'd imagined.

The maire covered his eyes with his hand and squinted at the shop. "What have you done to my shop?"

Crimson's heart whirled, caught somewhere between the elation of bright colours and the maire's severe tone. "I painted it…"

"Our town is known as a serious trading post in the queendom. I will not have it mocked because some upstart newcomer decided to flout our planning permissions and choose a garish," he shuddered, "yellow."

"I think it's cheery," Dilly said, lending Crimson her support.

The cunning look of someone who loves bureaucracy glinted in Maire Bowan's dark eyes. "Well, we shall have to review this choice of colour with the planning committee. They will be in touch, Miss Brouderer." The maire stomped off.

Hardy gave an apologetic shrug and trailed after the satyr.

Stitches. The last thing she wanted was to make an enemy of the maire.

"Very bright, Red. Very you," Lief said.

Crimson decided to take that as a compliment. "Thank you. And thank you for the help." Unless he'd wanted to set her up to get into trouble with the maire?

Another wink and Lief bent to his fiddle once more, striking up a jaunty song.

Crimson brushed down her dress and welcomed people inside for cakes and refreshments, courtesy of the Cozy Lobster. She had just stuffed a small brownie in her mouth when a shriek rang through the street.

A tall cat person appeared in the doorway, clad head to foot in a pumpkin orange dress with black stripes that contrasted with the neat rosettes on their fur. A matching hat with a long orange feather capped off the outfit and added another foot to their height.

Crimson put on a shopkeeper's smile, trying to work out how she knew this spotted felinix.

"Darlings!" The cat person elongated their vowels and added a purr to the 'r' so it came out like a low caress. "This is too much! Who is responsible for this beacon of fashion?"

"Er, me. I own it," Crimson said.

The cat person swept a bow, causing the hat to wobble precariously. "Runcible La Chat, at your service. But my friends call me Sibby."

"Sibby? From the posters?" That was why the cat person looked familiar.

"You've heard of my little show. How marvellous! Have

you seen it?"

"I've been a bit busy."

"But of course you have. Creating this haven. I have longed for something like this in our hometown."

"You live here?"

"Only when I'm not on tour. I'm back for two nights before I head off to the capital. The stage waits for no person."

"What sort of show do you have?"

"Quicker to ask what I don't do, darling. I am a performer." Seeing Crimson's blank look, they gave a toothy smile and elaborated. "I sing, dance, do acrobatics, even juggle balls." They gave a wink. "If you ask nicely."

"Cake?" Crimson proffered the tray, unable to think of a reply. Outside, she thought she caught Lief's smirk through the window.

"I couldn't. I haven't eaten sugar since, well, a lady never reveals her age." Another wink. "And I have to maintain this body." Sibby elongated the last word as they rubbed their hands down their perfect hourglass figure.

Too perfect. Crimson noted the padding that must sit around their hips to even out their shape and create the illusion of curves. But they liked colour. The orange dress said that much.

"What can I do for you Miss Sibby?"

"Miss? Oh no, that will never do. Don't constrain me with labels. Sibby is fine, darling." They patted Crimson on the cheek with a soft hand, the pads of their fingers light with wisps of silky fur poking through. "Now let me look."

Sibby inspected the dresses styled on the mannequins that Ig and Hardy had found for her. "The colour, I love, but the dresses…too everyday. Can you put a slit in them?" Sibby thrust out their leg to show off the slit cut up to their mid-thigh in the orange outfit.

"I can. But you'd lose the pocket on that side."

"I need to think, darling. But I'll take one of those headpieces. The bow is too cute, a little small for my liking, but I'll make it work. I can make anything work."

Sibby paid and left. "I'll come again, darling. Once is never enough." Another saucy wink and they were gone.

Hamlet slunk in later that day, meeting Ovelia with such an exaggerated comment of "Fancy meeting you here," that Crimson knew it was prearranged.

She smiled as they browsed, and Hamlet declared he would purchase a headband to match the eyes of his love and selected a periwinkle blue from the display. He shared a loving look with Ovelia, which turned to terror as his mother appeared in the doorway.

"There you are! I thought you were taking a while on the delivery rounds."

"Got to support a local business, Mum."

"Hmmm," Greezi sniffed and surveyed the shop. "Nice enough, I suppose. Too fancy for me, though. Hurry up and get back before the lunchtime rush." She left without acknowledging Ovelia.

The dwarf sighed and left too.

"Relationship problems?"

Hamlet sank against the counter. "Alas, my love grows frustrated that we cannot share our desire with the world. So, do we declare our love and risk our parents' anger or continue in hiding and risk fair Ovelia's ire? 'Tis a tragedy that we play out. And I cannot see a way forward."

"And you're sure your parents would be so against a match between you two?"

Hamlet gave her a look, then barked a burst of brittle laughter. "You jest with me. If my mother were to learn of our trysts, she would force me to swineherding duties for the rest of my days. To say nothing of what she might do to my love. Oh, what to do?"

He sighed.

Crimson thought for a moment. It was a conundrum alright. "How about a romantic gesture?"

Hamlet's head snapped up with a spurt of decisiveness. "Yes, a gesture. But a headband is too small for the largeness of my love." He crumpled the bag in his hands. "I need a token as bright as your shop." He snapped his fingers. "That's it! I shall paint our shop to show Ovelia that my love burns bright enough that I shout it from the rooftops with paint."

"Will your mother be happy with you painting the shop?"

"In truth, my taking an interest in Hambrosia will please her so much, she will not question my motivation. Now I away, to select a colour that best signifies my love for fair Ovelia."

Crimson watched him leave, dodging past Dilly, who had arrived with a new batch of cakes. The baked goods proved more popular than Crimson's clothing. That wasn't distressing at all.

The petalborn passed her a mug of steaming tea. "Lavender and chamomile. To help calm you and give you perspective."

"I don't need tea," Crimson replied as she took the cup. "I need sales."

"Hush now, everything works out."

Crimson would normally agree with the sentiment, but as the day wore on, she sunk deeper into uncertainty.

The shop saw plenty of footfall that day as the entire town trooped in to see the new addition to their high street. A few people bought headpieces or fabric bracelets she'd made with scraps; the cheaper items. But nobody wanted a dress.

People examined the clothes, liked the pockets, but balked at the colour and the price. At this rate, she'd have to accept piece work to make ends meet.

At the end of the day, Crimson leaned on her counter and sighed.

"You can go now. I doubt anyone's going to come this late." Crimson offered the band what remained of the cakes and they dived in with a ravenous hunger that made her think she never wanted to be a musician.

When not a crumb remained, they packed up their instruments and left. Lief took his time packing his fiddle away until he was the only one left.

Crimson held up her hand. "Don't say it."

"Say what?" He looked bemused. But her feelings were too fragile. She couldn't take whatever teasing he wanted to dish out.

"I don't know. I thought this place would love bright colours. People make such lovely material here. But no one seemed to be interested. The only things I sold were accessories. I thought people would want my vision."

"Did you ask anyone what they wanted?"

Crimson scoffed. "You don't understand fashion." She gestured to his plain shirt and trousers.

Lief sucked in a breath and hoisted his fiddle case over his shoulder. "Stop trying to foist your ideas on the town and listen to what people actually want." With that, he stalked off with an angry set to his shoulders.

Crimson slammed the door behind him. How dare he presume to tell her what to do? She was an experienced dressmaker with ideas. She didn't need advice from a woodsman, of all people. She'd left her home to come here and share her designs with people, to draw inspiration from the bright colours of this vale. If she strayed from her vision, she might as well have stayed in Juniper Vale and become a piece worker for her old mentor.

Crimson snorted her annoyance. He couldn't understand. He had no ambition. Just because he was content to live in a cottage in the woods with no interaction with anyone, didn't mean he could judge other people.

She wanted the queendom to see her spark, her unique vision. It wasn't her fault that the people of Saffron Vale didn't value her designs. Maybe she should have chosen a busier vale, one with more hustle and bustle. A city like the capital rather than this backwater berg where she'd wasted her time and her money on creations no one would buy.

And yet…a treacherous voice in her head said that he was right.

She had whirled into this town, expecting a riot of colour and open-mindedness to her innovative designs, and the only sale she'd made was to a fashion-forward singer.

A flash of silver in the corner of the ceiling caught her eye as the luck spider settled back on its web. A word glistened in the fading light: *Listen.*

Maybe success wasn't about changing everything and forcing her designs on people. Maybe there was something else she could do.

Chapter 28

~ *Return to Wyrm Rock* ~

A WEEK LATER AND CRIMSON'S shop was still not the success she'd dreamed of. People came in, intrigued by the painted exterior and looked around, marvelling at the clever colour combinations. But the visit ended with muttered excuses; 'Too bright for me…' '…where would I wear it?' 'I like the pockets but…' 'if only there was something more subtle…'

She had added more, smaller accessories that she made in the evenings, staying up and working by the light of a small candle. Ovelia had bought one of the green headbands with an oversized bow, but Sibby remained the main return customer, keen for accessories to work into their show.

What else could she do? People didn't want her clothes, so she'd made smaller, more affordable things so they could add a pop of colour to their outfits without needing to buy an entire dress. But that covered the rent and nothing more, and even then, only because it was so cheap.

Her creativity had its limits, and she was out of ideas. She spent her days doodling, hoping that something would strike her, but her well was as empty as her shop. It was at the end of one such disappointing day when an unwelcome visitor showed up.

The bell rang as the man entered, its cheerful ring a taunting refrain of failed sales. But still, Crimson looked up and smiled on instinct and sheer wilful optimism, until she recognised Lief's unmistakeable frame.

"It's you."

"It's me." He smiled, and Crimson gritted her teeth. He looked like a predator, and that meant she was the prey. She wouldn't play that game.

"What do you want?"

"I thought you were always nice to people, especially customers."

"Are you going to buy anything?" She folded her arms across her chest as she called his bluff.

He looked down. "No."

She scoffed and returned to her book. Accounts and designs were the only things she had to do, and without sales, her accounts were more depressing than ever as the money frittered out. To compensate, her designs became more elaborate, as if her brain wanted to rub in the fact that her concepts just didn't sell.

It didn't matter where she was, here, or in Oasis, or anywhere else in the queendom, maybe she wasn't cut out for success. But she was darned if she'd show that to Lief.

She ignored him as long as she could, and when it was clear that he wasn't going to leave, she looked up and with a sigh of irritation asked, "What do you want then?"

"I thought you might like to visit Smudge."

Crimson's heart skipped a beat and all her petty anger vanished. "You'd take me?"

He shrugged. "I'm going anyway. Need to collect some seaweed. I could take you. If you want. But I'm going now."

"Yes! I mean, yes, please." Of course, she wanted to see Smudge. His absence had left a dragon shaped hole in her heart. And she'd even tolerate Lief if she could have a few moments with her lost friend.

"Come on, then." Lief walked out of the shop and started down the High Street.

Crimson scrambled to follow him, forgetting her cloak and pausing only to lock the door before she scurried after him.

The pace he set left her breathless, and it wasn't until she was in the boat that she had a chance to speak. She reached over and placed one of her hands on his, waiting until Lief met her gaze, and she said, "Thank you."

He nodded and starting rowing, his cheeks flushed with the effort of pulling the oars. Crimson's gaze snuck from the horizon to Lief.

She had tried to nurse hatred for him for making her leave

Smudge on this desolate rock, but something had changed during the cheese rolling, or maybe when he'd brought her flowers, or the picnic they'd shared, and she found her thoughts turning to him more than they should. That was natural, though. If you hated someone. Her fingers plucked at a flake of paint as she puzzled through her feelings. At the very least, she couldn't hate him anymore, not after he'd given her this chance to see Smudge again.

They pulled into the same cove as before and Crimson scanned the cliffs, expecting Smudge to come running to her.

But there was no sign of the small purple dragon.

"Smudge! Here boy!" She made kissy noises with her mouth and shaded her eyes to better see.

A few dragons lifted their heads from where they lay stretched out on the rocks, but none came over.

"Maybe he's not here," Lief said.

"Nonsense. He's not in the cove, that's all. I need to get up there." Crimson started for a steep path etched into the bristling heathers.

Halfway up, she realised her mistake. The path was more treacherous than she'd thought, and thorns snagged her dress until she looped half of it through her belt, creating makeshift trousers that left her calves exposed to the vicious spikes.

But she kept going. If she could see Smudge again, feel his warm, reassuring scales against her fingers, she would know that she'd done the right thing by letting him go. And she wanted comfort. Some way of knowing that she belonged in

Saffron Vale. And the little dragon could give that to her.

So Crimson struggled on, ignoring Lief's shouts of warning from the ground, until she stood atop the cliff.

A dragon flew past, its cinnamon wings buffeting her. Crimson pinwheeled her arms as she pitched backwards. And, after a few terrifying moments, she righted herself.

"Smudge! Smuuuuudge!" she called.

From up here, the view was incredible. The sun hung as a golden orb just above the horizon. The twin moons – one a waxing crescent, the other a waning gibbous – etched in white against the darkening sky and Ig's lighthouse shone in the curve of the coast that marked Saffron Vale.

But Crimson's focus was on the dragons. There were creatures of every size and colour, from sparkling blacks through to opalescent whites with every colour of the rainbow in between. And there, a flash of purple.

Crimson tiptoed through the dragons. "Sorry – pardon me – just going over here."

One of the larger creatures snapped at her ankle, but it was a warning and she backed away, weaving towards the purple as smaller dragons shifted out of her way and slithered over her leather boots.

When she got to where she thought the purple had been, she called again, her eyes searching for her familiar dragon.

She couldn't see him anywhere. No lolling tongue. No playful nuzzle against her legs. No contented purring growl. Crimson turned to go, and her gaze lit on a single midnight purple scale on the ground. She clutched it tight in her palm and straightened.

Though nothing changed around her, in her mind, the dragons seemed more menacing than before, with sharper teeth and pointy claws. A flash of fire bloomed in the corner of her eye, and she backed up. A whine and growl told her she'd stepped on a tail.

What if they turned on her? These dragons were wild creatures, not tame pets like her Smudge. Still on tiptoe, she raced back with an agility she never dreamed she possessed, through the horde of dragons to the path where she slid and slipped her way down, uncaring of the gorse bushes that pricked her legs.

At the bottom, she tripped on a rock and went flying, arms outstretched. Crimson closed her eyes, bracing for the hard collision with the ground.

Instead, strong hands caught her and lifted her onto the sand. "You could have got yourself killed!"

"What do you care?" Crimson's voice came out in a bitter bite. Her Smudge was gone, leaving only a small scale and the memory of his skin under her hands.

"If you'd listened, I brought food. Maybe we could sit and eat and wait for him to come to us."

Food. Of course. Smudge loved eating with her. She was such an idiot not to think of that, and Lief had thought of everything. Crimson breathed, noticing she was still in Lief's arms, and his hands were warm even through her woven dress.

"Thank you," she whispered, stepping back and taking in the picnic blanket already set up in the centre of the sandy beach.

"Shall we?"

Crimson nodded and accepted Lief's arm of support, allowing him to lead her over to the same rough spun blanket they'd sat on last time they were here.

She lowered herself to the floor, noticing that her calves were still on display and bloody from the spiked plants.

"Here." Lief took off his shirt and handed it to her. Crimson's breath caught in her chest. "For your legs."

"It'll ruin the linen." Blood stains were a nightmare to get out.

He shrugged, as if it was nothing. She opened her mouth to protest again, knowing he was so poor he had to mend his own boots, but he turned away from her and started unloading the basket. The subject was closed.

Crimson took the shirt and dabbed at her wounds. It wasn't as bad as it looked. Most of the bleeding had stopped, and she unhitched her skirt from her belt and covered her legs, feeling shame flood her. She had acted like a fool.

As they ate, Crimson twisted around, searching for Smudge. She left an entire pork pie in the hope that the small dragon might come back. But the only creatures interested were the flies and tiny dragons that crept up to the blanket, hoping to steal some crumbs.

"How's the shop going?" Lief's voice sounded forced, like he wanted to project a cheerfulness that neither of them felt.

"Do you really want to know?" Crimson sighed and drew in the sand with her finger, the soft, white grains warm with the last heat of the day.

When he stayed silent, she decided to be honest. What did she have to lose? He already thought she was an idiot; it wasn't like she could sink lower in his estimation.

"Not well." She let out a hoarse laugh. "Terrible, actually. People come. They love the paintwork – thanks for that by the way – and say nice things, but sales are small. Maybe coming here was an awful idea."

"Maybe."

She shot him a look. The whole point of unburdening yourself to someone was to get comfort, not to feel worse. "Helpful."

He sighed. "I don't know much about shops. But I know people don't like things that are forced on them–"

"I'm not forcing anyone!"

Lief rubbed his hand over his forehead. "I mean, have you asked people what clothes they want?"

Crimson stared at the sand and added another line to her geometric design. She always thought better when her hands were at work, and this was a lot to think about.

After a long silence, Lief nudged her with his boot. "Time to go. Unless you want me to leave you for the night."

She narrowed her eyes at him, ignoring his last comment. "But Smudge hasn't come yet."

"Maybe he won't come." Lief's eyes were kind, and his

words were soft as he spoke the truth that Crimson didn't want to hear.

She hugged her arms around her stomach. Smudge didn't want to see her. He'd forgotten her in such a short space of time. She was alone.

"I guess I'm just unlovable."

"You're not." Lief's voice was rough, but his words were enough to shock her out of her selfish spiral of sadness.

"Why are you being so nice to me?"

He shrugged and a smirk crossed his face. Crimson frowned and opened her mouth to ask what was funny. With a swift tug, Lief pulled the picnic blanket out from under her, sending her sprawling onto the soft sand. Back to normal, then.

They started for the boat when Crimson jerked to a halt.

"You don't really want me to leave you overnight, do you?" Lief asked, not breaking his stride.

"You haven't collected any seaweed."

"What?" His brow creased in confusion.

"Seaweed. That's why you said you needed to come here."

"Yes, yes, that's right."

"Where's your basket? I'll help."

"Here." Lief held up the picnic basket.

Crimson's nose wrinkled. It was a practical solution, but why hadn't he brought a basket specifically for the seaweed instead of reusing the carrier? The boat didn't have a lot of storage space, but any future food would have the lingering whiff of seaweed.

Lief bent and grabbed what looked like random strands of seaweed.

And what if she'd said no? He'd brought enough food for two. Or maybe he'd brought his dinner and shared it with her. She had no idea how much he ate.

With a start, she rushed to join Lief. "Are we looking for any particular type of seaweed?"

"This type." Lief held up a thick, dirty green piece.

"But you've got different ones in there already."

"Are you a seaweed expert now?"

"No." Crimson backed off and roamed the shore, searching for the thick rubbery seaweed he'd pointed to as the sun lit the sky into orange fire.

Chapter 29

~ Curvy carts ~

NOT LONG AFTER THE disappointing trip to Wyrm Rock, Crimson received an official letter from the maire's office, notifying her that the bright paint on the exterior walls was a breach of planning permission. In convoluted words, it gave her a period of ninety days to repaint it in one of the appropriate muted colours from a palette ranging from white all the way through to cream or face a fine.

She took the morning off from her deserted shop and sat in the corner of The Cozy Lobster musing on her failings, starting with her designs that didn't sell and ending with her lamentable lack of knowledge around the planning process.

Dilly set a mug of hot chocolate on the table along with a slab of saffron cake, a small round chocolate and a glass of water.

"New recipe," the petalborn grinned as she stood back and waited for Crimson's review.

Crimson sniffed the chocolate, wary after the chilli incident. The confection had a delightful combination of sweet and salty aroma that made her mouth water.

Satisfied there were no nasty surprises, Crimson bit into the hard chocolate shell, allowing the dark bitterness of the chocolate to melt on her tongue. A soft cream came next, a gorgeous, sweet texture that dissolved into the taste of fish.

Crimson gagged and glugged down the water.

"Too much?" Dilly pouted. "I thought it might be overpowering. Duncan said it was alright, but he'll eat anything with chocolate on it."

"What fish was it?" Crimson gasped between mouthfuls of water. Fish and chocolate, what an awful combination.

"It wasn't fish. As if I'd put trout in a chocolate." Dilly rolled her eyes. "It was seaweed."

That explained the taste. "Not something I'd expect to find in a sweet."

"That's the point. I want to create a surprise. A unique blend of chocolate with something else. But it's no good if only me and Dunc can enjoy it." Dilly's face perked up. "Oh well, back to the chocolate slab. I'm so glad you're my taster; I can trust you to be honest."

Crimson wasn't so sure she wanted the honour of being Dilly's taster if this was the outcome, but she couldn't say no to the friendly petalborn. "Speaking of honesty, can I ask you a question?"

Dilly motioned for Crimson to get on with it. A troll perused the cake selection, and, while extensive, the choice would only keep them busy for so long.

"What sort of clothing do you prefer?"

"Still not selling?"

Crimson sighed. "No, and I'm beginning to think my designs aren't what people want."

"Your dresses are fabulous. I want one, but…they're expensive." Dilly held up her hands. "I know, I know. And it's right they are; you've put your heart and soul into them. But I don't buy a new dress every month and most folks here wait until their clothes wear out before getting new ones."

The petalborn tilted her head in thought. "What I wouldn't mind though, with winter coming up, is some stockings." With that, Dilly left before the troll started drooling on the display.

Stockings…Crimson noted that down in her book and took a sip of her hot chocolate. The soothing warmth of the liquid filled her soul, or maybe that was the new ideas bouncing around her head. Who could tell with chocolate?

Invigorated by talking to someone, she decided to ask more potential customers and made her way to Hambrosia as soon as she'd finished her cake and drink.

Hamlet grinned at her from by the counter.

"Decided on a colour for the shop, yet?"

He sighed, his face taking on a melancholy air. "I cannot

choose. Which is fairer; the pink that matches my love's lips or blue for her eyes?"

"Does your mum know you're painting the shop for Ov–"

"Shhhh! Do not speak that name here. My love must remain a secret from my family, lest it become all-out war. We shall steal our kisses, making a mockery of fate."

"Not this again." Hamlet's mother leant over the cut window. "He can't shut up about this new girl, but he won't tell me her name. What's the matter, hey? Ashamed of your old mum?"

Hamlet rolled his eyes. Of course he was embarrassed by her; he was a teenager.

"You don't know who it is, do you?" Greezi eyed Crimson.

"Er…"

"Thought not. What can we get you then? Bacon for your dragon?"

The sudden lump in her throat at the mention of Smudge threatened to choke her. Crimson forced it down and aimed for a smile. "He's not with me anymore."

"Typical man, leave you in a heartbeat. That's why I've told Hammy he's not to lead anyone on. It's all right for him to dither around while he's young, but if it's serious he's got to be all in. No making promises he can't keep."

Hamlet shot Crimson a forlorn look. She sympathised. He'd given his heart to Ovelia, all in. There was just the small problem that she was the daughter of his mother's rival.

"If you're not here for meat, what do you want?"

"Yes, er, actually, it's about my business."

Greezi raised a bushy eyebrow.

"I know you came into the shop, but you didn't buy anything, and I was wondering what you would be interested in."

The orc let out a snort. "Lady, I work in the back all day. I don't need anything fancy to fry bacon." She thought for a moment. "But those pockets were useful. Can you put them on anything?"

"Yes, as long as the fabric's thick enough."

"Well, I'd quite like pockets, especially on an apron, but those bright colours. I mean, why would I wear them? Who have I got to impress?"

"You could wear them for yourself."

Greezi jerked back like Crimson had hit her. She shook her head. "For myself. Hark at you. I don't have time to think for myself, what with running this shop and worrying about Hammy. For myself, indeed. Now, are you sure we can't get you anything?"

Crimson bought some ham for her dinner, feeling an obligation after Greezi had given her so much to think about.

As she plotted her next move, thoughts of work aprons with pockets spiralling through her mind, she noticed people streaming down the High Street.

Ovelia danced past her, and Crimson smiled as she saw the flower headpiece in her hair. She reached out and touched Ovelia's arm.

"What's going on?"

"The Lobster's on the beach." Ovelia pronounced the capital letter.

As if that explained anything. Crimson wanted to ask more, but Ovelia moved back into the crowd, buzzing with excitement. The girl made sure she moved past Hambrosia's window, slowing her walk and swinging her hips. Hamlet appeared, disappeared back inside, and then both he and his mother joined the throng.

Crimson smiled as she saw Hamlet move up next to Ovelia in a nonchalant way that could be accidental. If you didn't know they were madly in love. Such a sad circumstance.

Someone jostled Crimson, and she realised she stood in the middle of the street. She stepped to one side and decided to join the crowd. It was a town event and she needed to understand more about the community she now lived in.

"Out of the way! Clear the way!" A loud shout came from behind, accompanied by the thud of hooves on the hard ground.

Crimson turned and saw the maire driving a cart pulled by two oxen. Hardy sat next to him, gripping the seat and gritting his teeth. And behind the first cart was another that bounced from side to side. Pedestrians scattered, pressing themselves against the walls.

The maire pulled to a stop near Crimson, the back cart jinked at an angle with the first one. "Alright, everyone in."

No one moved.

"Come on, do you want to see the Lobster or not? This will get you there faster and save your legs. Ah, Crimson, our newest entrepreneur, join me." Maire Bowan gestured to the carts, which had bench seats along each side.

Crimson looked around for help to refuse the maire's request. He had a lot of nerve to invite her to ride with him after that darned letter.

"Actually, I wanted to talk to you about the fine."

"You got the letter? Capital. But I can't discuss individual cases in the open. You'll need to make an appointment."

"Then, can I do that?"

The maire gave a world-weary sigh and rubbed the back of his furry neck. "I don't know. I'm a busy satyr, lots of duties and such. Enough to drive you to distraction. But if you were to take a trip with me, maybe I could move some things around…"

The bribe was clear. But Crimson didn't want her obituary to read 'Died in a road accident when she was foolish enough to ride in a bonkers cart'.

"Er…" Her gaze swept the street, looking for support, for any excuse not to ride.

Lief strolled by, unconcerned by the cart parked in the middle of the street.

"Lief, our eponymous warden, you'll come for a ride?"

"I'd rather walk."

"Come on, too chicken for a hardy dardy, are you?"

Lief stiffened, but he shook his head. "Not even a dare will get me in that death trap."

Titters of laughter rippled through the crowd of spectators, who had moved closer now the crazy cart was stationary.

Maire Bowan's brow creased.

Crimson straightened her spine. The maire's bizarre transportation might look odd, but she embraced change, and she didn't like how Lief dismissed his ideas. Besides, she had a fine to discuss. She took a deep breath. "I'll get on."

"Excellent!" Maire Bowan pulled a lever and a set of steps descended near the driver's seat. Crimson climbed aboard and took a seat.

"What do you call this?"

The maire patted his wooden seat with pride. "This is the curvy cart. Double the carrying capacity of a single cart, but you only need the same number of drivers. That's economy. Now, get in the back for the best experience." Maire Bowan shooed her down into the second cart.

Crimson hesitated before shuffling down. At the place where the two carts joined, there was a thick lining so she couldn't see the street under her feet as she hopped into the back cart.

"Only a fool would trust that thing," Lief said, staring at Crimson with a smile playing around his lips.

Why did he enjoy needling her so? Every time she thought they might be friends, he'd make fun of her or say something like that.

"Better a fool who lives life than one who never takes any chances." She was quite proud of that retort.

"Anyone else?" asked the maire.

No one else chose to join her.

"Right then, away we go. Hold on to your seat."

Chapter 30

~ *The Lobster speaks* ~

ESPITE THE SLOW PACE of the oxen, the back cart jerked with violence, careening from one side of the road to the other as they proceeded down to the beach.

Pedestrians hugged the walls of shops as they passed. Crimson would have felt embarrassed if she hadn't been so concerned with holding on for dear life. Every slight dip in the road sent the back cart in another direction and jolted her so hard she was sure she'd fall out. She'd started the journey sitting upright, but after the second corner, she ended up gripping the edge of the cart, twisting in her seat to press her body against the side, wincing with each bounce.

The maire pulled the cart to a screeching halt by the low stone wall butted up against the rocks to form a natural separation between the sand and the firmer land. It took

Crimson a moment to steady herself and ease some of the tension from her muscles before she felt able to leave the cart.

"What did you think? Invigorating, hey?" Maire Bowan asked with a gleam in his round eyes.

"That's one word for it."

She caught Lief's eye as he loped past her, heading for the steps that joined with the jetty and led to the beach. He had an I-told-you-so expression on his face, so she had to say something.

Crimson raised her voice. "I'm sure it will be a great success." As long as the passengers were thrill seekers with no care for comfort. "Perhaps some straps to help people hold on might improve the ride for people not used to the motion."

The satyr's face crinkled. "Really? Wouldn't that take away from the fun? But I suppose if it encourages people to use it… Hardy! Take a note; straps for the back cart. Capital idea."

"Wait!"

Maire Bowan turned back.

"The appointment? To discuss the," she lowered her voice as she realised people had turned to stare, "ahem, letter."

"Ah. Well, if Lobby's here for the reason I think they are, I can't possibly meet until after the harvest. What do you think, Hardy?"

The clerk flicked through a leatherbound diary and nodded. "You should be free directly after the harvest." He shot a wink at Crimson.

What did that mean? Was he on her side? Hadn't the letter

come from the clerk?

"Well, if that's sorted," the maire rubbed his hands together, "let's see what old Lobby has to say for themselves."

Crimson followed in the maire's wake down onto the sandy beach, unable to get an answer as to when exactly the meeting was. Maire Bowan disappeared into the crowd, using his hooved feet and elbows to carve a path to the front.

Crimson cursed her small stature as it was soon clear that there was no way she'd see anything from the back of the crowd, and she lacked the maire's audacity to push her way through. Sometimes she wished her teg blood hadn't made her so petite, after all, it wasn't like she had inherited any magic along with her size.

She settled for scrambling up a seaweed covered rock so she could see something. And there, right at the spot where the foamy surf met the wet sand, was the same gigantic lobster that she'd encountered with Ig. They loomed over the cove, casting a long shadow over the sand as their enormous form blocked the sun.

As if her thoughts had summoned him, Ig glided down from his striped lighthouse and perched next to Crimson, smoothing his feathers and peering down the beach.

"Ah, I thought it'd be this week. I've studied the weather patterns."

Was she supposed to know what he was talking about? "What's going on?"

At that moment, the maire bleated to get everyone's

attention. "Everyone, it is an auspicious time. The Great Lobster is here to talk to us, and I know we're all keen to hear what they have to say. So, I give you, our Great Lobster, old Lobby themself."

The Great Lobster's eyes narrowed at the nickname as a loud round of applause sounded around the cove before dying down to an expectant silence that stretched on.

The maire swayed, shifted from hoof to hoof, looking at the enormous lobster with growing impatience but with too much respect to speak again.

Crimson wondered if the Great Lobster enjoyed this small annoyance of the maire.

And then the crustacean spoke. Its low, sonorous voice vibrated through the rocks and echoed off the cliffs. For a moment, Crimson doubted if this was the same crustacean, such was the resonance of their tone, but the mottled spots of purplish blue on their shell were unmistakeable.

"Good people of Saffron Vale, I bring good tidings."

A satisfied murmur ran through the spectators.

"There will be a squall tomorrow and then the weather will be ripe for the planting and growing of the saffron plants. I will return with news of the harvest." With that, the lobster heaved itself back into the briny sea, disappearing beneath the waves.

Maire Bowan clapped his hands together. "Excellent. You all heard the Great Lobster, guardian of our vale. Hardy, tell them the plan."

The clerk stepped forward, his voice clear. "Anyone with a plough team, please come to the fields straight away so we can prepare. Then, as soon as the rain's finished, we can plant the bulbs overmorrow."

Everyone nodded and the murmurs this time rang with purpose and agreement. People headed back up the steps, and the crowd dispersed.

"That's it?" Crimson looked around, wondering if she missed something.

Ig nodded with a sigh. "The traditional way of starting the saffron season. I've been trying to convince people we can decide ourselves by measuring the weather, but the maire won't move away from the lobster tradition."

"Speaking of the maire…he's…well…" How could she finish that sentence when people had voted him in?

Ig waved their hand, dismissing her concerns. "The maire here is more of a ceremonial position than anything else. We found that Bowan caused much less trouble in an office where he has all the pomp but little real power than if he were in a role where he actually had," Ig shuddered, "responsibility.[4]"

Crimson furrowed her brow. It made some sort of sense.

"And since he loves tradition, I expect we'll never move away from the Great Lobster deciding our saffron season."

"Does he always stick to tradition? He's got this curvy cart—

---

[4] If you think this is far-fetched fantasy, look around at some of your local politicians. Go on. See?

"

Ig snorted out a hooting, wheezing laugh. "That thing! He's obsessed with it. I keep telling him the idea won't work, well I mean, practically it can work, but no one in their right mind would use it. The back cart is far too unstable, unless you join the two to make an extra-long vehicle, but then how could it manoeuvre around corners?" He wiped a tear from his eye and caught Crimson's look. "Oh no…"

"Oh yes. He's made one. I rode it down here."

"And?"

"It's awful, but I felt so sorry for him. And it was the only way he'd discuss my fine."

Ig scoffed. "That's no reason to support a bad invention. Do you know how many stinkers I've turned out? I'm all for experimentation, but there are some rules you can't bend, and some things you can't improve on. Like the wheel. I've tried all manner of different shapes, but nothing can beat a circle."

"Miss Brouderer! Miss Brouderer!" The maire's braying voice rang over the beach. "Your chariot awaits. Come, come."

"Er, I thought I might stay here and talk to Ig for a while." After all, the exchange was one ride for one meeting about the letter.

"Oh no, I've got to get back and check on the steamer. I've recalibrated the pressure gauge and reduced the size of the leaves."

So much for that idea. The tylluan was oblivious to social

niceties such as giving your friends excuses not to ride on death carts.

And there was Lief, standing at the foot of her rock, offering a hand to help her down. She took it, ignoring the buzz of heat that burned up her arm and into her stomach when they touched hands.

"I can save you," he whispered. "If you admit you're wrong and I was right."

Crimson held her head up high. "Never." She would never give him that power over her.

"Then enjoy your ride. See you on the other side…if you survive."

Chapter 31

~ *Saffron collecting is back breaking work* ~

THE GREAT LOBSTER HAD spoken again in the time old ritual and today was the day – almost exactly six weeks since they had gathered on the beach. The entire town gathered at the edges of fields carpeted with delicate purple blossoms. Crimson knelt next to one and tried to decide if it was more purple or lavender. A delicate floral scent wafted up from the field; part honey, part metal, and part sweet grass.

Ig found a spot next to her and clicked a contraption that reminded Crimson of a set of tweezers crossed with a grasshopper.

"What are those?"

"Good, isn't it? Three tweezers in one. Speed up collection in no time."

Crimson pulled out her own standard silver tweezers, provided by the maire on the condition that she returned them to the collective pool at the end of the season and paid for any breakages. She had then been informed that she probably wouldn't need to use the tweezers because she was assigned to the fields.

"I thought we picked the flowers?"

It was the only job the town had trusted her to do, and even then, she was under supervision. Hardy flanked her on the other side, ready to swoop in if she damaged any of the precious flowers. Separating the orange-red stamen from the petals happened in a tent set up a little way from the fields.

The maire stood on a stand close by and tapped his hoofed foot on the wood for attention. "Residents of Saffron Vale, these next few weeks are the most important of the year. The Great Lobster says that we have the perfect weather for picking and the rainbow trout have been spotted in the river, which, as we all know, portents a bountiful harvest."

A cheer went up from the residents. This was the focal point of their entire economy; three weeks of frantic picking, harvesting and drying with the profits shared among the town in a combination of coin and the spice itself.

Representatives from ATOZ sat in their own tea-coloured tent next to the dryers, delicate bronze scales at the ready to weigh the takings and pay handsomely for the freshest saffron.

"Now I know many of you think that I like the sound of my own voice," Maire Bowan continued, "but you'll be happy to know that I've decided to keep this brief. Ever since I took on the honour of the maire-ship, I have strived to…"

"I'd better stop him before he starts listing his achievements," said Hardy, getting up and heading for the stand.

Crimson shifted on her knees, impatient to start the harvest and prove she was part of the town.

"You up for this, Red?"

She snorted as Lief took up Hardy's place next to her.

"I'm sure I can manage to pick a few flowers."

"It's not just the picking, it's how long it takes. Weeks of crawling across the dirt, making sure you don't damage the blossoms. I'm not sure you've got the hands for it."

Crimson held up one small hand. "I think my hands are better suited to plucking delicate flowers than your sausages."

"Ouch." He held up one hand next to hers and her heart skipped a beat as she felt the heat from his palm against hers. "Just don't give up too easily. I've bet you'll last at least a day."

"Pardon?"

"In the pool, to see how long you last."

"There's a pool?" Crimson's voice rose and several heads turned their way. She lowered her voice. "You mean to tell me that people are betting that I'll give up?"

He nodded and smiled an evil grin.

"But that's…that's…horrible." She stared at the dark

ground, her hopes for belonging draining into the mud. Why had she ever thought that she could be part of their community? No one was interested in fashion, they bet on the worst outcomes, chased cheeses and relied on lobsters for pivotal harvests. This vale lacked sanity or structure. And yet…and yet, she wanted to belong here, to prove she could succeed.

Lief tilted her chin up and her lips parted in surprise at the intimate gesture. "So, prove them wrong, Red."

Fire flooded her belly. She would prove the doubters wrong.

"…And that's why I want to focus on traffic…what?" Hardy nudged the maire in the ribs. "Oh right, let the saffron harvest begin!" With that, the maire swung a large, padded mallet, almost as tall as him, at a ginormous brass gong sending a booming ring across the vale.

On either side of her, people started picking flowers, loading them into canvas bags that hung from their sides. Crimson bent forward and began plucking the crocus blossoms.

"Not so hard. They want to be picked; you don't have to force them." Lief sighed. "I'll show you."

He demonstrated, and Crimson copied him.

"No, you're crushing the petals, see how the pollen falls from the stamen?"

Crimson looked at the bruised flower in her hand, now smeared with the bright pollen. "Stitches and pins."

"Here." Lief took her hand in his. Crimson froze at the sudden heat where his palm touched the back of her hand.

"Like this."

He selected a flower and pressed her fingers together in a soft pinch. The crocus head fell into her palm.

"See?" His breath warmed her ear and slow heat spread through her body, making her heart beat faster.

"Thank you, Lief, for looking after our newest crocus picker," Hardy stepped up behind them, rubbing his hands together.

"Someone had to." Lief's voice was rough and he released her hand as if it had burned him.

Crimson stared after him as he retreated to his own row of purple flowers, her heart still pounding in her ears.

"Come on then, lots to do. Stir your stumps, everyone!" Maire Bowan strutted along the field, urging the harvesters to pick faster and harder.

Ig gave her a knowing look. She glared back and shook her head. There was nothing between her and Lief. But Ig smiled a smug, irritating smile and gave a hoot of 'I told you so'.

So, Crimson waved at Milus a couple of rows over and said hello loudly.

The blacksmith waved, his metal hand glinting in the morning light as he returned her greeting and said 'good morning' to Ig, who blushed and put his head down as if his only focus was the flowers in front of him.

It was petty, but Crimson didn't want Ig's scrutiny, especially as she had no idea what had happened with Lief. They didn't like each other, so why did her eyes slide over to where he knelt among the blossoms, looking like some nature god? And why did her heart stop when he lifted his dark head to meet her gaze?

She turned back to her row and plucked crocuses for the rest of the day, refusing to look up from the purple flowers that stood proud in the mud.

This continued on the following day and the day after and Crimson got into a rhythm of picking, placing in the canvas bag that hung over her shoulder until it was full, before raising her hand to indicate she needed a new one.

Of course, Lief moved onto sack duty after the first day, so she couldn't ignore him as he replaced her full bag with an empty one and commented "Still here, are you?" before taking her haul over to the stamen sorting tent. It was infuriating, but she didn't have the energy to be angry because she was exhausted from the bending, picking, then inching forward for more bending and picking.

The only relief was at lunchtime when Maire Bowan rang the gong again and the harvesters all gathered at the buffet table set up near the dryers and laden with food.

It was there, a week later, that she got promoted to stamen sorter.

Chapter 32

~ *Promotion to stamen sorter* ~

CRIMSON LOADED HER PLATE with crusty bread, cheese, and one of the allotted pies for field workers. She bit through its thick, crisp crust and moaned at the combination of meat and apple sauce. Delicious.

"That good, hmm?"

Lief's voice sent goosebumps down her arm. What had happened to her this week? It must be something in the air, or in the pollen.

Crimson swallowed her mouthful and nodded. She wanted to give a cutting remark, but all she could think to say was, "Possibly the best pie I've had while picking crocuses."

"But not the best pie you've eaten?"

Crimson thought for a moment, then shook her head. He

smiled, that small smile where he didn't show his teeth that made him look oh-so-superior, and she knew he thought she was referring to their first meal together. So she took a moment to pretend to think, knowing just how to tease him and wipe that smug look off his handsome face. "I think the best pie I've had is the chocolate pecan in Oasis."

His face fell and inside, she smiled.

"I see." He looked at her with the strangest expression, then he blurted out, "And what about my pie?"

Crimson took another small bite of her meal and chewed as she thought. A wicked smile cut across her face. "It's in my top ten."

"Top ten?"

"Wait. I forgot about Marie's apple pie. Top twenty."

A flash of annoyance, and then amusement passed over his face. "Well, then I'll have to invite you back to mine for another try."

Crimson's face heated and she bent her head over her plate to hide her blush.

It was then that Ovelia appeared at the lunch table, wringing her hands, and asking for the maire.

"Are you alright?" Crimson asked, glad of the distraction.

"No, one of our sorters has taken ill. I've got to find Maire Bowan and Hardy. We're a pair of hands down and there's so much to sort."

"I'll help."

Ovelia grasped Crimson's free hand, meaning she could no longer eat her lunch. "Will you? Oh, thank you. Let's go check with the maire."

She dragged Crimson over to the second table where the maire was in the process of devouring his own meal while Hardy picked at a piece of bread, never far from the maire's side. The maire wiped away the crumbs from his neat, curled beard as he saw them approach and took a swig of cloudy apple juice from his cup.

"Lovely to see you, ladies. How are you enjoying your first crocus season, Miss Brouderer?"

"Very well, thank you," Crimson said, freeing her palm from Ovelia's and sneaking a bite of bread.

"Crimson's going to help us with the sorting. Billy's taken ill."

Hardy frowned and exchanged his plate for a clipboard. "Are you sure that's wise? No offense to Miss Brouderer, but she has no experience."

"Nonsense!" Maire Bowan cut in. "It's not like we have much choice and she's an extra pair of hands, a veritable boon of the season. Besides, look at these hands." At this, the maire snatched up her plate and held both of her hands in his own sweaty palms. "Regard these slender digits, and remember, she has ample experience with fine stitching. We shall transfer Crimson to the sorting tent!" He waved his arm at this last statement as if it were his idea all along.

"Ovelia, show her the process, and quick."

"But, my lunch–" Too late. Ovelia dragged Crimson to the dusky yellow sorting tent as Crimson looked longingly at the tables of food.

Inside the tent, the sweet smell of honey and grass overwhelmed her senses. The sorters laughed as they told jokes and gossiped while their hands moved with practiced motions over the tables where the soft purple flowerheads lay.

"Sit here." Ovelia shoved Crimson into a seat next to her. "Take a flower, separate the petals and stigma, put the stamen in this basket. There's nothing to it."

Crimson copied Ovelia's practiced motion and ended up with a smear of the golden pollen on her pale fingers.

"Gentler. You're trying to separate the stamen, not squash them. If you can't do it with your fingers, use the tweezers."

Crimson took a deep breath and tried again. As she worked, she entered the same state of mind as when she sewed and soon found a rhythm – a pinch, a twist, a pluck – and the stamen fell from the petals without the need for the long tweezers.

The woven basket lined with linen filled with the valuable stamen and someone collected it for transfer to the dryers who tended fires nearby ready to dry the delicate spice and even roast some for different colour and taste before giving it to the saffron assessors and then the ATOZ representatives.

It was a laborious system, but it worked. And Crimson sank into her part of it, determined to do well.

"Drink?"

"Please," Crimson croaked. Her throat was dry from the pollen that hung in the air despite the sorters' care, and she hadn't had the chance to grab anything more from the table. She drank deeply from the glazed pottery cup Lief handed her, cool water refreshing her mouth and throat.

Some dribbled down her chin and onto her plain, linen dress and she dabbed at it. "Thank you, that's very kind of you."

"Got to take care of all our sorters." Lief's voice sounded rougher than usual, and Crimson looked up to see a strange look on his face again. Then he coughed and headed off, offering drinks around the tent.

The pollen must get to everyone, she decided, turning back to the sorting.

Chapter 33

~ A successful sale ~

THREE WEEKS LATER AND Crimson sweated as she hauled the final box into place for her stall at the Crocus Festival. Yesterday, the town had finished harvesting the delicate saffron, and today was the start of the festivities. She stretched her spine, wincing as her muscles protested.

Picking through petals was easier than the back-breaking work of harvesting saffron, but sitting for hours in a hunched position, plucking stamen from the purple flowers cramped her back and her fingers ached, useless for sewing for at least a few days.

"I could sleep for a week," she declared to no one in particular.

"I'm impressed you made it this far, Red."

Crimson jumped. How did Lief manage to move so quietly? "I hope you lost your bet."

"Oh no, I won."

Crimson's face crinkled with confusion. "I thought you bet against me."

"I knew you were made of stronger stuff. I bet you'd make it."

Crimson's stomach flipped at the compliment, and, for once, she was lost for words. Before she could stammer out a thank you, Lief had moved on.

She unpacked the last box, arranging her stock with care when her fingers brushed something hard in the wooden crate. Crimson peeked into the box. And screamed. How in the queendom had that dratted pig-duck-demon monstrosity got into her wares?

She put it to one side while she finished sorting out her stall. Maybe she should get rid of it once and for all. There were plenty of bins around.

A cough dragged her attention from the ornament and to a potential customer. Crimson stifled another yelp, worried that her heart might not take any more surprises today. There, in front of her, stood a pale figure dressed in white. The ghost.

"Are you real?" Crimson asked, glancing around to see if anyone else had noticed the apparition.

"Are you wanting that?" The figure gestured to the ornament.

"No. Please, take it."

The figure smiled and pocketed the hideous ceramic creature before strolling into the crowd.

"Wait!" Crimson called after him. "What is it?"

The ghost shook their head. "It's a pig o'course. Me mam made it back when her gran lived in your shop." Crimson might have thought she'd imagined it if Ig hadn't interrupted her thoughts.

"Met Jiminey, have you? Surprised he's awake at this time of day. He works the night shift on one of the boats." So he was real. And that was why he'd only showed up at night. Ig handed her a mug of cloudy liquid. "Elderflower scrumpy, to celebrate your first saffron harvest."

He clanked his own mug to hers with a satisfying chink, and they both drank. Crimson sighed at the fruity, sweet taste of fragrant elderflowers mixed with apple. This vale had the best apple juice.

She finished her mug and asked for another, handing Ig some coins. "This round's on me."

"As you say. Take it easy with this stuff though." Ig headed off to get some more drinks.

***

The gong rang over the fields at midday, declaring the Crocus Festival open. Maire Bowan made a speech that thanked the harvesters before he rambled on about improving the traffic situation in the vale. Hardy coughed politely after the five-minute mark and Maire Bowan finished by telling everyone to enjoy themselves.

Crimson adjusted one of the stockings on her stall, her stomach reeling with nerves. Her big launch hadn't been a success, but she had spent every spare moment creating this new stock based on the feedback she'd gathered from the town. Today would either go well or she would have to slink back to Oasis and beg her former mentor to take her back as a piece worker. And everyone she'd grown up with would know she was a failure.

The butterflies in her stomach became huge birds as people started to mill among the stalls.

The most popular stalls were the ones with food and drink, as everyone celebrated the end of weeks of hard work.

The maire walked past, and Crimson scurried over.

"Maire Bowan! Please, you said you'd meet with me after the harvest."

The satyr's brow crinkled.

Crimson dug around in her pocket and pulled out the crumpled letter demanding that she repaint her shop.

"Oh, I can't deal with that now. I have to do the rounds." He patted his stomach. "Civic duty."

Hardy placed a hand on Crimson's sleeve. "Best to wait. You'll want the planning committee onside, anyway."

"And how can I do that?"

"Leave it to me."

Crimson still wasn't sure how much she trusted Hardy. The letter had come from the maire's office, after all. Didn't that mean the clerk had drafted it? But he headed off after the maire, his long legs meaning he caught up with ease.

Crimson smiled as a Greezi approached the stall. Even the owner of Hambrosia had closed her shop for the day to celebrate the harvest, although, like Crimson, she had a stall where Hamlet stood stealing glances over to the Eggselsior stand where Ovelia tossed egg salad with teasing flicks of her wrists.

Greezi thrust out her jaw and glared at the display on the stall. "Colours are bright."

"Yes, I wanted to showcase Saffron Vale's excellence with colour. Everything you see here is locally dyed." Crimson's mouth dried up as the orc ran a critical eye over a dusky pink apron with a carnation red pocket sewn on the front.

"Seems too nice to wear for work."

"It's hard-wearing linen and the darker colour on the pocket hides any stains it might get through use." Crimson smiled and tried to project confidence.

Greezi moved over to a set of stockings and ran her fingers over the fabric. "I suppose you haven't got anything in my size," she said, folding her arms.

Crimson eyed the large orc, measuring her up with a practised glance. "These should fit." She handed over a pair in a deep blood red. "Or I have them in cobalt or plain undyed, if you prefer. Perfect for the coming winter, double layered and there are matching garters." She decided to be daring. "Some people like to get a different colour for each leg."

"Alright, I'll have the apron."

Crimson smiled and folded it up. "Anything else?"

The orc's eyes darted from side to side as if she were nervous about someone seeing her buying undergarments. She pointed at the stockings. "I'll take the red."

Crimson took her money with a smile and wrapped the stockings in a neat brown paper package, tying a yellow ribbon around it.

"Thank you." The orc paused and Crimson waited for a stinging comment. "I'm glad you've moved here." With that, Greezi disappeared into the crowd. Crimson stared after her. That was unexpected.

As if it opened the floodgates, more customers lingered at her stall and most of them bought something; the stockings were her biggest seller, followed by the embroidered headbands.

Crimson smiled to see flashes of colour on the heads of the townsfolk. A small cough brought her attention back to the stall and her heart flipped.

An ATOZ representative stood in front of her, arms folded, face hard.

"Can I help you?" Crimson asked, smoothing down her dress and forcing her hands to stay out of her pockets.

"Is that dress for sale?" The troll pointed at the mannequin clothed in a deep carnelian red with a contrasting collar and pockets of saffron yellow.

"Yes."

"Do you have any more?"

Crimson kept her face professional as she'd learned during her training at Senda's shop in Oasis but inside, she wanted to dance.

"Yes, I've got several colours." Crimson dug them out of the chest she'd lugged up here and laid them on top of the stall so he could see.

"I'll take them."

"Really? I mean, of course. You do want all of them?"

He nodded. "We serve the entire queendom. The colours will do better in some vales than others, but I think they'll sell. What's your trade price?"

They negotiated and Crimson held her ground, charging what she knew they were worth in time as well as fabric. After five minutes, they were both happy and she'd made a tidy profit; enough to keep her shop open at least for now.

"And what do you call the collection?"

He thought this was good enough to be a collection. Inside, she screamed for joy. Only true fashion designers had collections. Her brain scrabbled for words, and she blurted out the first thing that came to her head. "The Pocket Collection." Not very original.

But the tall troll nodded and made a note in his book.

Ig returned with another two glasses of scrumpy, and

Crimson raised hers in a toast. "To success."

"You sold something?"

"All the dresses. I'll need more cloth. Are you dying any soon?"

Ig scratched his chin and pondered. "I suppose I could. I'm not sure if I can get a better dye though. Maybe I should turn my attention to fixatives."

"Your previous batch was perfect."

"Nonsense, we can always improve."

"Here's to that." They chinked glasses again and drank with satisfied camaraderie.

Chapter 34

~ *The planning committee* ~

I T WAS AT THAT point that the maire, his clerk, Duncan and Dilly, arrived at the stall.

"Miss Brouderer. I believe you wanted to talk about the colour of your shop," the maire said with a broad smile on his face.

"Er, yes." Crimson eyed the ATOZ representative, hoping he'd leave, but he seemed content to stay and watch her decisions get picked apart.

"Hardy suggested I bring the full committee along to speak with you." Maire Bowan nodded at Hardy, Dilly and Duncan. Her friends were on the planning committee. A tiny ember of hope flickered in Crimson's heart. But Dilly's face remained impassive, and Duncan stared down at the folded copy of The Golden Acorn newspaper in his hand.

"It is the duty of this committee to make sure that our town remains respected and upholds its valued position of commerce in the queendom. Now, I want to make sure this is factual. You decided to paint a long-standing building on the high street yellow without consulting the planning committee. Is that correct?"

"Yes, but–"

"And did you receive the letter informing you to repaint the shop or pay a fine?"

"Yes, but–"

"And have you repainted the shop?"

"No, but–"

"You still have time. Otherwise, we'll expect prompt payment of the fine. Fifty bums, wasn't it? That's gold suns," he added, making sure she understood.

Crimson blanched at the reminder. That wiped out all the profit from the ATOZ sale.

"And I am most upset that you have convinced impressionable young minds to consider painting their shops in unusual colours as well. Tut, tut, Miss Brouderer."

"You mean Hamlet? But–"

"The letter was sent in the name of the planning committee?" asked Dilly, cutting across her protests. Crimson hung her head. "I don't remember discussing it."

Crimson handed over the creased letter.

"It says the maire's office here," Duncan pointed at the seal.

"Not the committee."

Dilly scratched one lilac horn. "We haven't had a committee meeting in months."

"A mere detail. I strive to uphold the standards in the town, and I don't think we have more to say here. Either repaint the shop or pay the fine. I need another ale."

"That yellow shop is yours?" asked the ATOZ representative.

"Yes." Crimson hung her head.

"Brilliant idea."

"What?"

"What?" echoed the maire. Behind his back, Dilly, Duncan and Hardy shared a small smile.

"Great idea for drumming up more business by making the shop bright and welcoming. It's a destination. People might even come from neighbouring vales when they hear of it," the ATOZ representative said. "And I will make sure I mention it."

"Hmmm, well, regardless. It's an eyesore, taking away from the communal beauty of the town and damaging our reputation. And you are not on the planning committee."

"ATOZ," Duncan said.

"I beg your pardon?"

"The answer to this crossword clue. An organisation who prides itself on knowing trade inside out. ATOZ." Duncan pointed to the puzzle.

The maire snatched the paper from him. "An acronym! What has the queendom come to when the editor allows crosswords to have acronyms as solutions?" He shook his head.

"So, as the senior ATOZ representative here, would you say that mister…"

"Sniggens," supplied the troll. "At your service."

Duncan bowed to the troll. "Mister Sniggens knows something about trade?"

"I suppose." The maire glared at the crossword as if it had offended him.

"So, we should listen to his views about the impact on trade." Dilly said. "He said it might increase our commerce. If more people come to the town, that's more tourist suns to spend."

The maire squinted and tapped his hooved foot as he thought. Then he broke out in a grin. "Capital idea. Let it never be said that Saffron Vale does not support innovation in all its forms. I knew there was something special about you, Miss Brouderer. A glad addition to our wonderful community."

"So, the letter?"

The satyr took it and chewed it up, swallowing the paper as if it were a normal snack.

"Forgotten. Now, I shall write a letter about this acronym usage. The standards at The Golden Acorn have gone downhill since Blintze took over. Hardy! Take a note…"

Maire Bowan walked off, crumpling the newspaper in his hand and dictating a long-winded letter to the unfortunate editor of The Golden Acorn.

244

Chapter 35

~ *A welcome return* ~

A S THE SUN LOWERED over the sea, the crowd of people at the harvest festival got noisier, in part due to the joy of celebrating a successful harvest but for a larger part due to the cider and scrumpy that flowed from the drinks tent.

Crimson took a moment away from her stall, stretched, and enjoyed the view across the water. The festival had settled into a party atmosphere and fewer people were interested in clothes as the afternoon waned, focusing instead on food, drink and music. So she'd packed away her stock and decided to take a moment for herself before getting dinner and heading to bed.

She was so tired, the thought of dancing made her want to curl up at home, perhaps with a nice book from the travelling library that had arrived at lunchtime. Yes, a good fantasy book would be the perfect way to end the day. Perhaps with a little romance or a journey to a far-off land in search of treasure.

A speck crossed in front of the golden sun. A gull finding its way to roost, perhaps.

Crimson drank from her cup. The scrumpy was delicious. Why had no one told her about it before? They should sell it in The Cozy Lobster. She decided to tell Dilly as soon as she saw her. Maybe she should have it in her shop so people could drink while they browsed her wares.

Congratulating herself on an excellent business idea, she looked out over the horizon again. That dark spot was larger now. Something moved towards the vale.

Crimson shaded her eyes with her hands. It was such an unusual size. Bigger than a gull, but smaller than say a pegasus. She bit her lip. Should she tell someone?

She looked back at the field and her gaze lit on Lief's face. The warden would know what it was. And then laugh at her for her big city stupidity. Better to wait until she had a clearer view.

The thing kept coming, arrowing straight for the field. She squinted against the sun's rays. A crazy thought rushed through her, that whatever it was, it was coming for her.

She shook herself. How stupid. The effects of exhaustion after long weeks of harvesting and sorting saffron were catching up to her.

The sun was halfway under the sea now, its light dancing on the soft waves of the Southern Ocean, and the speck disappeared into the shadows of the early evening.

There. Nothing to worry about.

Crimson turned, ready to go back to her stall when a familiar low-throated purr rang across the sky accompanied by the flap of wings.

She span round, eyes wide as a dark shape collided with her sternum, knocking her to the floor and stealing her breath.

Through choking gasps and tear-stained eyes, Crimson blinked up at the small dragon, who sat on top of her, licking her face with a wet, pink tongue.

Smudge!

The dragon lay on her stomach and stretched out, the warm heat of his scaly body sinking into Crimson as she cuddled him to her.

"You came back. You came back." Crimson breathed out the words, not believing that her wildest dream had come true; her companion had returned.

Smudge gave a snort as if to say 'of course, I'm back,' and sniffed the air.

Crimson recovered and pushed herself up to a sitting position on the spongy grass. Clutching the dragon to her, she stood, cradling him in her arms, fighting against her muscles, which protested that she wasn't strong enough to carry the dragon for long.

"You must be hungry."

Another snort of agreement. Crimson laughed, a grin spreading across her face. Today was a perfect day.

Chapter 36

~ *A truce* ~

CRIMSON WALKED BACK TO the harvest fair, giving up on carrying the wriggling dragon as soon as they reached the first stall.

In the darkening night, small lanterns lit the festival in a soft muted yellow, reminiscent of the saffron the town had collected.

At first, she worried that he might run amok and cause havoc, but the dragon must have missed her as fiercely as she missed him because he stayed by her side, so close to her feet that he tripped her up at least three times.

Crimson bought him several steaming slices of the best back bacon while Greezi cooed over the small animal. Hamlet was far too cool to fuss over a dragon, but he slipped in a scoop of burnt ends on top of the order when his mum wasn't looking.

Smudge accepted it all with happy snaps and greedy slurps before he headed over to a bale of hay and settled down. Crimson nudged him off, mindful of the damage a single spark from the small dragon could do. Smudge grunted but curled up near the stage instead.

Dilly sank down next to her and handed her a large slice of apple cake. Crimson whispered her thanks and took a bite, sighing with pleasure. It was the perfect thing to accompany the scrumpy. Speaking of.

"Do you mind watching Smudge while I get another cup?"

Dilly nodded and pulled out a small box from her bag. "If you'll try this chocolate."

Crimson froze. Oh no. But she couldn't get out of it. She reached for the chocolate cup, studying the cream inside. It was too dark to see the colour and her nose filled with rich caramel. Oh well, down in one.

She forced a smile onto her face and put the chocolate in her mouth, chewing it fast to get it over with.

"Mmmm," she mumbled through a mouthful of chocolate. "That's great. I mean, really good."

"Do you really like it?"

"Your best yet." Then all moisture in Crimson's mouth dried up. "What is that?"

"Did the seaweed come through?"

"It really does," Crimson sputtered, resisting the urge to wipe at her lips.

Dilly rewarded her with a full grin, exposing pointed teeth.

"Have another."

"Maybe later."

"And I'll have a cup of scrumpy. I need something to help me put up with Duncan's blathering. He's worried there won't be enough pumpkin pasties. People can always have the apple pie, but he won't be told."

Crimson smiled and went to get the drinks, not sure how apple juice could help Dilly. A familiar voice ordered over the top of her head.

"Excuse me, there is a queue." Righteous indignation poured out of Crimson as she glared at Lief.

"Ah, but band members get served first."

"You're not part of the band."

"Want to bet?"

"I'm in too good a mood to argue. Just get your drink and go."

Lief quirked an eyebrow. "And what's caused this good mood? Dare I think it's bumping into me?"

"As if." Crimson grinned from ear to ear. "Smudge is back."

His eyes widened.

"I know you don't think it's right that he's with me. But he's made his choice. He came back. So there. And I'm making him a harness, so he'll be safe for next year's cheese rolling." She folded her arms, preparing for an argument.

"I've never known a wild creature choose a person before." Lief gave her a strange look that she couldn't interpret.

"Well, maybe you don't know everything."

"Clearly."

Crimson sighed. "Look, I know you don't like me. But how about a truce for tonight? I don't want to argue, I just want to enjoy the festival."

His eyes sparkled and in the half light of the lanterns, they almost glowed. "Alright. Truce."

They shook hands and Crimson blamed the flip in her stomach as their skin connected on the cake she'd eaten.

"I do know that you're too uptight to enjoy the party, though." A smile softened his teasing words.

"I was enjoying it. Until you showed up."

"What happened to our truce?"

"Sorry." Crimson clamped her mouth shut, annoyed that she'd apologised to him. Why couldn't she resist snapping back? It was like he brought out the worst in her. Or maybe it was something about the vale. That she could be herself without hiding the parts of her that didn't fit in, that would have made her old mentor's eyes boggle and get her sent to bed without supper.

"How about a dance?"

"What?"

"A dance. You do know how to dance?"

"With you?"

Someone shouted his name over the crowd. "Ah, I've got to go. I'll find you later."

Crimson nodded, struck mute by his offer. She got her drinks and headed back to where Dilly lounged on the hay bale. Lief surprised her with his talk of truces and dancing. So any thought about telling Dilly her good idea about serving scrumpy at the café fled her mind.

Instead, she downed her drink, feeling the warming fuzziness of the apple juice fill her. Strange. Juice didn't normally have that effect. Maybe there was something in the air.

Epilogue

~ Lief takes Crimson home ~

IEF SPUN CRIMSON ROUND again, noticing the flush in her cheeks. She was so alive, so vibrant. It almost made him wish he was better with people. But any time he got close to someone, they left.

Better to keep his distance and focus on the forest and protecting the natural diversity of Saffron Vale and not get distracted by a petite dressmaker with pretty eyes. Even if she had agreed to dance with him.

"You're staring." Her speech slurred as she flung the accusation at him.

He didn't know what to say. How could he tell her that he was trying to work out what colour her eyes were? Were they fern green or more forest green or salamander green like the lizards that flitted around the forest he called home? And those rainbow flecks twinkled like magical stars in a moonlit night. So he kept quiet and instead raised his eyebrows into a questioning expression.

"Whazza matter? You think I can't dance?"

Lief's lips quirked up as her words blurred, taking the sophisticated edge off her Juniper Vale accent.

"I'll show you." She didn't need him to reply in this one-sided conversation. That was the problem with scrumpy, well one of the problems. It did tend to make people argumentative. Although, maybe that was just Crimson. He seemed to bring out a side of her that no one else saw.

Truth be told, he liked it. So often, people were scared of him because of his size or what he was. But she didn't care about that. She just wanted to be loved. He knew it the same way he knew how to breathe.

And that scared him to his soul. Because he couldn't love her. He couldn't get close to her. He couldn't risk losing her like he'd lost everyone else he cared about. It had happened with his parents, when they died. Then, as soon as his younger sister came of age, she'd left for the capital.

Away from his brooding thoughts, he realised that Crimson had let go of his hands. He clenched them at his side, resisting the impulse to gather her to him.

Lief frowned and tilted his head as Crimson did a strange jig. She danced like her feet were on fire, with furious concentration on her small face. Her hair flew round, the lanterns catching the reddish tint within the brown. People stopped to watch the energetic display, cheering and clapping as her stockinged feet tapped like they were filled with otherworldly fervour.

Maire Bowan joined in, stomping his hooved feet with gay abandon. At the fringe of the crowd, Ig tapped his foot in time with the beat, his eyes on the minotaur strumming the guitar on stage.

Crimson stopped with a sudden flourish and a kick of her heels and gave a triumphant "Ha!" before swaying.

He caught her as she stumbled. "I think that's enough dancing for you."

"Nonsense. I can go all night."

"Aye, I'm sure you can. Let's go over here." Lief herded Crimson over to a quieter spot on the edge of the dance floor.

"I don't feel so good."

"Do you want to sit?"

"No."

"Alright, let's slow down then."

Crimson nodded and stepped close to his chest, leaning her cheek against him and swaying to an internal beat that bared no resemblance to the frantic tempo of the country music that surrounded them.

Lief swallowed. He moved them further into the shadows, unsure if she'd want the gossip that would follow them in the small town if they were seen slow dancing, but unable to stop moving with her.

He let her lead and their bodies rocked together in an intimate rhythm. He tried not to think how nice it was having her close. Instead, he focused on breathing and keeping her upright as she rocked them from side to side.

Breathing was a mistake. The warm, soft scent of her filled his sensitive nose. Apples and linen and something sweet, unique to Crimson; vanilla and spice. Intoxicating.

"You're alright, y'know that?" she murmured against his chest.

He pulled away, not sure what she wanted or what he wanted. Never mix scrumpy and feelings.

"How much have you had to drink?"

"S'jus pple juice."

"Scrumpy isn't apple juice. It's alcoholic." That explained everything. She hadn't realised she'd been drinking and had imbibed more than she was used to.

"Izzit? Then…" Crimson pulled away and her face creased as she counted off on her fingers before giving up. "Lots."

"OK, you need some water. Stay here. I'll get you some."

Lief made sure she was sat down, safe from the vertigo effects of too much good scrumpy and headed back for water. He bumped into Ig, still staring up at the Milus on stage.

"Why don't you ask him to dance?"

Ig hooted and fluffed his feathers, disturbed from his private reverie. "What? Who?"

"Milus. You should ask him to dance."

"Don't be ridiculous. He's playing with the band. I couldn't interrupt. Anyway, I was musing on the amplifying properties of different woods…"

"Of course. Look, Crimson's not feeling well. I'm taking her home, have you seen her dragon?"

"Mmm?" Ig's gaze had wandered back to the stage. From the glazed look in his eyes, Lief knew he had stopped listening. If Lief were a betting man, he'd wager than Ig was focused on the blacksmith playing the instrument rather than the guitar.

"Never mind."

Lief got some water then searched in earnest, avoiding the rest of the town out celebrating the harvest. He cocked his head, listening but the music was too loud to hear any noise a dragon might make, even with his sensitive ears.

Old fashioned searching it was. He circled the dance floor, praying the dragon hadn't wandered off and wondering how long he could leave Crimson until he stumbled over the small creature dozing by a hay bale.

Smudge hissed up at him.

"Sorry, but you are sleeping on the floor where anyone could trip over you."

The dragon blinked up at him as if to say that no one else had trod on him.

"I said 'sorry'. Now, come on, we've got to go. Crimson's had too much to drink."

With a snorting humph, the dragon came with him. Lief

hurried around the back of the stage, taking the quickest and quietest route back to where he'd left Crimson. But when he got to the spot, she wasn't there.

He cursed and closed his eyes, blotting out his vision and focusing on his other, keener senses. A full moon approached, and his inhuman gifts were almost at full strength. He inhaled, breathing in Crimson's sweet scent and when he opened his eyes, an amber glow flashed over his irises.

She hadn't gone far. If he strained his ears, he could hear her singing a soft lullaby as she wandered to town.

He raced after her, not trusting anyone under the influence of scrumpy to make it home alone.

"Crimson," he called so as not to frighten her.

She lit up as she turned to greet him, and his heart skipped a beat. No one here looked at him like that. Like they were happy to see him for no reason. "You're here. And Smudge came too! He came back to me, y'know." She waggled her finger at him. "So, you were wrong. He's not wild. He wants to be with me."

"I told you to wait at the festival."

She shrugged and started walking again, weaving across the path. "Why's the road moving?"

"That's the scrumpy."

"Don't like it." She stopped, wavering on the spot before falling to one side.

Lief caught her with ease. She made no move to right herself.

His stern expression melted as she gazed up at him with those trusting rainbow-flecked eyes. He could lose himself in them, if he let down his guard. And that frightened him more than a rogue unicorn.

When she spoke, her words were a whisper, but clearer than they had been. "Not sure I can make it home." Crimson's eyelids fluttered closed.

"Don't fall asleep."

"I know your secret."

Lief froze. He kept his voice perfectly even as he asked, "And what would that be?"

"You can paint. You painted my shop, and you painted that picture in your cabin."

He exhaled. Thank the moon that was what she meant. As he searched for a reply, a soft snore came from her rosebud mouth. "Oh, for moon's sake."

People had started to meander back to Woolton. He could hear them coming. And they would see her unconscious in his arms and jump to conclusions. Rumours would race around the Vale. He didn't mind; he could stare them down. People already talked about him behind his back. But Crimson…she wanted to fit in, to call this place home. It would destroy her burgeoning confidence if people whispered about her.

A fierce need to protect her rushed through him. Lief tried to rouse her. He shook her, patted her cheek, called her name in a shout whisper. She gave a small snore. It was the cutest thing he'd ever heard.

Lief shook his head. He couldn't think of her as cute. He shouldn't think of her at all. He should take her to her house and leave her well alone.

But it wasn't like Smudge could take care of her if she woke in the night, vomiting up the contents of her stomach. Ruddy city girl drinking scrumpy like it was apple juice.

Lief made his decision. He scooped her up and, cradling her like a newborn deer, carried her to his home.

***

Thank you for reading A Colour to Dye for. If you'd like to read Lief and Crimson's meeting from his point of view, you can find free bonus chapters here: https://books.gemmaclatworthy.com/colour-to-dye-for-bonus – there's so much Crimson misses!

You can also get the prequel to Crimson's story and find out why she decided to move to Saffron Vale here: https://books.gemmaclatworthy.com/a-dress-with-pockets

Thank you

A special thank you to my amazing patrons: Emma Ward, Mark Canty, ZomBev and Sueann Snow, who always support me.

If you want to support Gemma, you can find her on www.patreon.com/G_Clatworthy for exclusive first reads of new stories.

You can also join her newsletter at www.gemmaclatworthy.com for a free prequel to her Rise of Dragons series and follow Gemma on www.instagram.com/gemmaclatworthy, www.facebook.com/gemmaclatworthy or join the Facebook reader's group Gemma's book wyrms.

Other Books by G Clatworthy

Books in the Saffron Vale series:

A Colour to Dye For

Going for Guild

Commission Impossible

Books in the Rise of the Dragons series:

Awakening

Solstice of Dragons

Equinox Betrayal

Darkest Deception

Attack on Avalon

Fated Bloodlines

Eat, Pray, Dragons

Magical Liaison Office short story collection

Books in the Omensford series (set in the Rise of the Dragons universe):

Bedsocks and Broomsticks

Cream Teas and Crystal Balls

Donkeys and Demons

Pumpkins and Popstars

Exes and Enchantments

Fae and Familiars

Gnomes and Necromancy

Children's Books

The Child Who series:

    The Girl Who Lost Her Listening Ears
    The Boy Who Lost His Listening Ears
    The Girl Who Dreamed of Sleep
    The Boy Who Dreamed of Sleep

Nanny Pastry series:

Nanny Pastry and the Nimble Ninjabread Man

Other books:

Coronavirus in the words of children

About the Author

Gemma started writing during the 2020 lockdown and loves fantasy fiction and dragons in particular. She lives in Wiltshire with her family and two cats and also enjoys crafts of all kinds. You can read all her writing first on www.patreon.com/G_Clatworthy.

Or join the conversation at Gemma's book wyrms readers' group on Facebook.

She also writes children's books. You can find out more on her website www.gemmaclatworthy.com or follow her on Instagram (www.instagram.com/gemmaclatworthy) or Facebook (www.facebook.com/gemmaclatworthy).

www.gemmaclatworthy.com

www.ingramcontent.com/pod-product-compliance
Lightning Source LLC
Chambersburg PA
CBHW051255210726
48287CB00002B/520